# DEATH
## COMES CALLING

## Book 6

The Death Card Series

By
## J.S. Peck

BEJEWELED PUBLISHING

LAS VEGAS, NEVADA

Bejeweled Publishing
6480 Annie Oakley Drive, Suite 513
Las Vegas, Nevada 89120


ISBN: 978-1-7368837-0-9
First Edition: July 2018

COVER ART DESIGN: Kelly A. Martin
INTERNAL DESIGN: Jake Naylor

# DEDICATION

I dedicate the entire Death Card series to my talented sister, Judith Keim, who has taken time away from her successful authoring to help and support me. "You have been the wind beneath my wings by believing in me and my talent for writing mysteries. When I've been in doubt, all I've had to do was pick up the phone, and you'd patiently share advice and encouragement. I honor and love you as my twin sister—I'm forever grateful."

I dedicate the Death Card series to all my beloved readers who have lived vicariously through the main characters of my books: Rosie, Isabella, Mike, Brian, Jack, Grandmother, all the sister-friends, Grandfather, Maria and her family, Coyote, Tom Little Horse, and all the others. I hope you've enjoyed the journey as much as I have in bringing them to you.

# Table of Contents

# CHAPTER 1

L ooking into the mirror, I bypassed the middle-aged woman with wild salt and pepper hair staring back at me and, instead, visualized my younger self with my beauty intact, who'd made choices that today I might not have made.

"That's hindsight, you silly woman. And who says you wouldn't have made the same choices today? Consider what they've brought you," I whispered to my image. Lost in thought, I didn't hear them until they were nearby.

"Where's your grandmother, baby girl?" a familiar voice asked.

I listened to the pattering of small feet as a tiny girl ran into my room. "Gramma Rose, it's me! It's Joslin!"

I opened my arms wide to receive the bundle of energy of my favorite granddaughter—my only granddaughter. I smiled at my daughter with her flowing dark hair and mesmerizing dark eyes, who was still as beautiful as she had been when I first laid eyes on her. She had been my little sister in a previous lifetime and now was my daughter in this one. I marveled at our exquisite reconnection.

"Isabella, love, when did you get here? Have I been dawdling?"

"No, Mama, I'm early. I couldn't wait to begin our day together. We don't often get to do that, just the three of us," she said as she kissed my cheek.

"Me, too," demanded Joslin as she clambered onto my lap. She sat facing me, placing her small hands against the sides of my face and kissing each of my cheeks. "I love you, Gramma Rose."

My heart filled with tenderness for her as I struggled to place her on the floor and rise out of my chair.

"Here, let me help you, Mama," said Isabella as she extended her arms to help me up.

"No, sweetheart, I need to do this myself," I insisted. I'd had a knee replacement several months earlier, which still gave me occasional discomfort—especially getting up after sitting for any time.

"Is this a bad day for you?" she asked with concern.

I smiled at her. "No, it's a perfect day to spend with my beautiful daughter and granddaughter."

As we neared the front door, Mike came forward. "Ah, my beauties, where are you off to?" He studied me, trying to remember what I'd told him earlier.

"We're going for cookies and sweets, Papa Mike," answered Joslin.

"That's right," he said with a chuckle. "High tea at the Waldorf Astoria, right?"

2

I smiled at him and nodded. He kissed my lips, lingering a bit, kissing me twice. He turned to the others. "Have a good time. I'll see you later, ladies."

"What are you up to, Mike?" Isabella asked.

"I'm watching the golf game on television at home."

"Good for you, Mike, a quiet afternoon without us," Isabella said, kissing him goodbye. I overheard her whisper to him, "I'll take good care of your woman; don't you worry."

He chuckled. "See that you do, sweetheart."

Mike was still striking with grey, nearly white hair, dark eyes, and his body in good physical shape for his age. As before, he stood tall and walked gracefully and confidently. We'd had many years together and became inseparable in heart and soul. It was a love that had endured the ups and downs of life and become stronger in time. It had not been so sure in the beginning...

*** 

We spent our first summer separated since our relationship had formed back then. By the end, we'd reached the point where we needed to decide how we wanted our relationship to move forward ... if at all.

Mike had returned to Boston to work at the detective agency he'd started with his business partner, Brian. They'd hired a female employee determined to win Mike's love at whatever cost, and our relationship had faltered. I'd spent the summer in Santa Fe with Isabella on her school break and had unexpectedly fallen in love with Tom Little Horse, who had been my husband in a former lifetime. In this life, he'd ended up being murdered, and I had been devastated. When I discovered I was pregnant, the baby's father could have been either Mike or Tom. I would remain silent about the baby unless Mike wanted our relationship to move forward and get married. I would not allow my pregnancy to interfere with his decision—or mine.

So, it was a great surprise at the end of that summer when Isabella and I returned home to Las Vegas to find Mike waiting for us at the airport with open arms. My heart lifted at seeing him, yet, I dared not believe that all was right between us unless I heard him tell me what I needed to hear. Only later, when we were alone at home, Mike and I had a chance to discuss our situation.

Mike apologized for his behavior in Boston, leaving me free to develop a relationship with Tom Little Horse. We shared what'd taken place with both of us, with my leaving out that I was pregnant. Only after Mike declared his love for me and his desire to spend the rest of our lives together did I tell Mike that he would be the father of a son. With my psychic abilities, Mike never questioned the gender of the baby, and so it was that the world turned right for us. Mike, Isabella, and I were ready for a new beginning... which now included a baby.

# CHAPTER 2

T hat day seemed so long ago. Yet, it still brought a smile to my face …

When Isabella returned home from her friend Sammy's that night, she sought us out, concern on her brow. She looked at me, and when I smiled broadly, she knew all was right with Mike and me.

"So, you're going to be a big sister, huh?" Mike asked. I chuckled to see Mike get up and grab Isabella in a hug.

"Yes, I can hardly wait!"

"Me, too, and I know you're going to be the best big sister of all time," he stated earnestly with a smile.

Isabella grinned at us.

"I agree," I said, nodding.

"What room will be his?" she asked, knowing we were using all three bedrooms already.

I looked at Mike. "I think we need to start looking for a new house. What do you think? Something to call your own?"

His face lit up. "That sounds good."

"Let's move close to Grandfather," Isabella said.

"Well, we can see what's available there, but …."

"There's one right next door to him, Mama. I saw it."

Mike and I looked at each other. Used to our psychic ways by now, Mike nodded in agreement.

The next day, I called Sylvia, the same realtor who'd sold the house to Grandfather. "Hi, Sylvia. I don't know if you remember me, but you were the realtor for Cal Williamson."

"Of course, I remember you and your darling daughter. What can I do for you?"

"We'd like to look at the house for sale next to his."

"I don't have one listed there unless it's in process, and I don't know about it. I've been off for a few days. Let me look."

She came on the line several minutes later. "Wow, you were right. It's not officially on the market yet, though. We're still taking pictures of it."

"Is there a chance we can look at it now—as is?"

"Let me check, and I'll call you back."

When Sylvia called back and said we could look at the house at four o'clock, I immediately called Cal to let him and Virginia know what we were doing and asked if they wanted to take the tour, too.

"Yes, for sure. Why don't you stay for dinner? We haven't seen you all for so long, and I'll put some steaks on the grill," Cal said.

"That sounds wonderful. Mike loves a good steak, and so do I. Isabella does now too. She has grown to like a lot

6

of things outside of pizza. I wasn't so sure that would ever happen," I chuckled.

"I know what you mean. That girl sure does love pizza. It'll be good to see you all. Virginia and I have missed you," Cal said.

At a quarter to four, Mike, Isabella, I, and our dog Sweet Pea drove into Cal's driveway and exited. Isabella ran to Cal, who stood in the doorway with Virginia. "Hi, Grandfather and Virginia! We're moving next door to you!"

Cal turned to look at me with a smile. "Is that right? How nice it'll be to have you nearby."

Cal, too, was used to our psychic ways and accepted Isabella's proclamation as fact. Then, he stepped down and held his hand out to shake it with Mike, standing stiffly at my side. I knew Mike was embarrassed by his previous behavior with Allison. That had been on full display at the time of the restaurant's opening, named after me. Mike hesitated momentarily before moving forward and clasping Cal on the back as he shook his hand. "Cal, it's great to see you and Virginia again."

"I'm happy to see you back where you belong," Cal whispered to him, speaking as a father might to his son.

"Happy to be here," confirmed Mike.

"Mama, there she is! The realtor is here!" announced Isabella. "Let's go and see our house."

I hugged Virginia, and then Mike kissed her on the cheek before we headed to the house next door. Mike took my hand, and we hurried up the walkway, looking at the beautiful home from the perspective of critical potential buyers.

After taking our time to look at everything downstairs, we made our way upstairs. Isabella stood at the top of the stairs with a wide smile. "Come look at my room and the baby's room, Mama. They're perfect—even the colors!"

At her words, we all stopped where we were. I turned to face Cal and Virginia, and Mike put his arm around my shoulders. "We were going to tell you over dinner. We're expecting a baby. You're going to be grandparents again," I explained.

"It's a boy!" said Isabella.

It was a moment to remember. We stood there beaming at each other, delighted with the news. Cal kissed me tenderly on the cheek and then shook hands with Mike. "Congratulations, son!"

The house was everything we could have asked for— 5 bedrooms, 3 ½ baths, a den, office, mudroom, laundry room, living room, dining room, and an oversized eat-in kitchen. The backyard was beautiful, with desert plantings. There was a Jacuzzi, a large covered patio with an outdoor fireplace, barbeque, and television. It had a place where we could clear an area to provide a private walkway from our backyard to connect to Cal and Virginia's backyard. The thought of having easy access to each other pleased us all.

# CHAPTER 3

## Present Time

*II* Mama, we're here. Let the valet help you out, okay?"

"I can do it myself," I said, rejecting her suggestion. One look from Isabella and I added, "But I won't."

I was stiff from sitting, and it felt good to move around. Before I got out of the car, Joslin began to pull on my arm. "Hurry, Gramma Rose."

"Joslin, don't pull so hard on her," commanded Isabella.

"Okay, Mommy," Joslin answered, dropping my hand and running ahead to wait for us on the veranda.

"You know how much I love that girl of yours," I said to Isabella with softened eyes.

"She feels the same about you, Mama. She's always loved you best," stated Isabella.

9

"After her parents, you mean," I said, smiling.

Isabella smiled back and nodded. "Yes, no one could ever replace her father."

"C'mon, let's go and enjoy our time together with your beautiful daughter, shall we?" Looking at Joslin standing there, I was struck by her beauty. She was a later-in-life gift from the Universe. She took after her father with her blond hair that waved naturally around her stunning face with large blue eyes that missed nothing. Her complexion was light like Sammy's, and the two together made for a fascinating look at how gene pools manifest.

We entered the hotel, the three of us attracting attention from those around us. I laughed to myself when I heard one of the bystanders ask, "Who are they? Aren't they movie stars or something?"

We were used to the attention and didn't respond or act upon it. We were simply three generations of women out for high tea and enjoying being together.

"How are things going with you, Isabella?" I asked. "You've taken on a big load when you and Sammy took over Cal's house. What does your husband think about that?"

"Thank goodness, Sammy is the type of man who realizes 'if the queen is happy, so is the court.'"

I chuckled. "Sammy's a smart man."

I watched Isabella's eyes follow a young woman as she passed by and sat down not too far from us. "Now there's trouble," she said.

I felt goosebumps cover me and a flutter in my stomach.

"Isn't that the woman who complained about the guest house used by transients?" I asked Isabella.

"It certainly is," she answered, annoyed. She gave me a look that indicated we'd discuss it later.

10

"Ooh, what are you going to eat first, Joslin? The biscuits or the sandwiches?" I asked.

"I think I'll start with the cookies," Joslin answered, eying me with a sly grin. I smiled and watched Isabella roll her eyes.

We finished our tea, and Isabella drove me home. Mike must have heard us as we pulled into the driveway because, suddenly, he was there. He'd come through the open doorway and stood at the end of the driveway waiting for me. His eyes lit up as he watched me walk toward him. It amazed me that we still were excited about being together even after so many years. My heart fluttered each time I saw his reaction, and warmth spread through me. I was a lucky lady. We stood with arms wrapped around each other and waved goodbye to Isabella and Joslin as they backed out of the driveway and headed next door, where they now lived in Cal's former house.

\*\*\*

Later that night, while I lay fully awake, sleep evading me, I looked at Mike, resting peacefully. He seemed so calm and collected, without worry. I smiled when I remembered that he was anything but when Mike and I were to marry in Santa Fe during the Christmas holidays. One thing after another seemed to go awry. I chuckled, remembering it…

"Where did you put that slip of paper, Rosie? You know the one—the receipt from the jewelry store in Santa Fe?"

"Didn't you take it out of your wallet to call them?" I hollered from the bathroom where I was applying my makeup.

"Yes, I did. They said all I'd need to do is bring them the receipt, and there'd be no problem."

"I guess we better find it then."

Mike looked frantic. "Isabella?"

She came running into our bedroom. "What is it, Mike?"

"Did you see the paper receipt that I had earlier?"

"You mean the one over there on the floor?" she asked, pointing to a spot near the bed.

"That's the one, alright. Thank you," Mike said, ruffling Isabella's hair. "Okay, listen up, girls. The cab will be here in less than an hour. Is everyone packed and ready to go?" he asked.

"Almost," Isabella said. "I just need to pack up Sweet Pea's stuff."

"Do you need help with that?" I asked.

"Nope. I've got it covered."

I went to Mike's side. "Are you okay? I've never seen you so uptight."

"Well, I've never gotten married before," he defended, pulling me into his arms.

"At least not one you remember," I amended, pinching his cheek.

"Ah, that," he grinned. "What a mess. I'm glad the girl's parents were understanding and gave us their blessings."

"Me, too."

Mike stuffed the receipt into his wallet. Noticing me lost in thought as I watched him, he asked, "What is it?"

"I can't believe that piece of paper has been through so much. I almost threw it out several times, thinking it had no value. When I showed the slip to the clerk at the jewelry store at the time of Karen's wedding, I thought he was talking about the bracelet you'd given me at Christmas last year. He said that I could come back to have it adjusted. I had no idea the slip had anything to do with an engagement ring. I can't believe you bought it a year ago."

"Last Christmas didn't feel like the right time to ask you to marry me, what with Coyote's nephew being murdered. I didn't want his death to blemish a happy time for us."

"I know. It's been a crazy year for all of us—good and bad."

He kissed me. "The good part is on its way. I know we're going to be happy together—all of us," he said, patting my belly.

"I agree," I said, placing my hand against his handsome face. "I love you, Mike."

"I love you, too, my queen."

Before long, the cab was outside honking its horn. Mike carried our suitcases to the car while Isabella and I checked the house to see if we'd left anything behind. We'd be gone for nearly two weeks while we spent Christmas and New Year's in Santa Fe.

During that time, Mike and I would be married. It wouldn't be the grand ceremony that Karen and Coyote had, but it would be perfect to have my larger family there. Mimi and her chef boyfriend, Charles, were staying in Las Vegas to run Rosalie's restaurant (named after me) so that Romano and Randy could take the time to attend our wedding. Grandfather and Virginia would be there, along with my sister-friends. Of course, so would Maria and her family—now my family, ever since Maria and I shared the role of being a mother to Isabella. Certainly, Grandmother, Angel, and Nica would be there as well.

Instead of wearing the beautiful heirloom Indian wedding dress that Karen wore for her wedding, I'd be wearing a maternity dress that my stylist, Louie, had designed for me. It was a stunning off-white silk flowing dress I could easily have adjusted to wear again after the baby was born.

Mike was standing over the open door of the taxi, waiting for us. "Hurry up, girls! Time's a-wasting."

I sensed I needed to look back as we pulled away from the house. When I spotted a lone suitcase on the doorstep, the cab had already begun to pull out onto the main street. I yelled for the driver, "Stop! We need to go back!"

The cab made a U-turn, and Mike got out and grabbed it. "Sorry. I can't believe I missed it."

We arrived late at the crowded airport. People in line were unhappy with us as we moved in front of them to reach the ticket window so we wouldn't miss our flight. My heart pounded with worry as we got close to our gate and heard them announce the last call for Santa Fe. As we raced forward, I wasn't sure we would make it on time. I relaxed only when all three of us, plus Sweet Pea, were seated on the plane. I sure hoped this wasn't a sign that the next two weeks would continue to be off-kilter.

Coyote was there to meet us at the airport. Karen was too uncomfortable with their baby due any day for the hour-long drive from Albuquerque to Santa Fe and back again.

"How's Karen feeling, Coyote?" I asked.

"She's uncomfortable right now—ready for our little girl to introduce herself to the world," he replied with a smile. "We can hardly wait."

"Have you decided on a name, Uncle Coyote?" asked Isabella.

"Sarah Lightning Foot," he answered.

"That's so cool," Isabella said.

"Why Lightning Foot?" Mike asked.

Coyote laughed. "Karen said that Sarah keeps running in her womb like she's trying to escape."

We chuckled.

"Karen is at your house waiting for you. She's turned up the heat and got you some groceries. She said you could settle the money with her later, Rosie."

"Gosh, I can't wait to see her! She said she's as big as a house."

Coyote nodded. "She's pretty big."

I patted my stomach, which was mushrooming. Isabella reached over, placed her hand on my baby bump, and smiled. "He's kicking up a storm, Mama."

"He sure is," I agreed.

Coyote pulled into our driveway, and I felt at home. More and more, Santa Fe was becoming my place of refuge. Tom Little Horse flashed in my mind, and I took a deep breath and pushed away sorrow at the thought I wouldn't see him again. I'd loved him, and it was too painful to realize how different things would have been if he'd lived. I was relieved that my love for Tom hadn't dimmed my love for Mike. Instead, in an unusual way, it made me value Mike even more.

Once home, Karen opened the door to greet us, a broad smile spreading across her face. Sweet Pea ran ahead of us to be the first one to reach her. But unlike other times, Karen could not bend to scratch her ears in greeting. Sweet Pea looked at her, then at us, in confusion. We all laughed at the dog's obvious unspoken question, "What's up with her?"

Karen hugged Isabella and then me. "Oh my, girlfriend, you sure look ready to have this baby," I said.

"In another week," she announced proudly and stepped back to let us inside.

15

"Sooner than that, I think," I whispered to no one, having seen a vision of her in labor.

"You're going to be there with me, Rosie?"

"Of course. I wouldn't miss your home birth for anything."

# CHAPTER 4

T he following morning, Mike got out all the Christmas decorations we'd stored in the shed, and Isabella helped me display them around the house. At the end of last year's season, we'd found a stunning, large, antique Santa Claus figurine made from leather, feathers, and wool blankets on sale. We placed it atop the fireplace mantle, which loomed large, becoming the centerpiece in the living room.

Tomorrow was Christmas Eve. Cal, Virginia, Romano, and Randy were flying in tonight and staying at the Eldorado Resort Hotel and Spa. After Christmas, Brian (Mike's business partner) would fly in to be Mike's best man.

Once again, we invited everyone to our house for a Christmas Eve buffet. I was looking forward to it. It should be a relaxing time since there would be many hands to make light of any work required to feed us all. I had ordered two pre-cooked spiral honey hams, and I'd already thrown together two casserole dishes and stored them in the refrigerator. Maria was making several Mexican dishes and flan for dessert. Karen was bringing three pies, and Grandmother and Angel were responsible for appetizers. No one would go hungry. Naturally, Romano would take over the kitchen activities and ensure everything flowed smoothly.

All day long, I felt anxious to wrap up all my Christmas chores as soon as possible. The feeling nagged at me, encouraging me to rush around. I made a mad dash downtown and picked up some of the items I'd ordered through the internet as Christmas gifts. It was exhausting to fight the holiday crowds, and I was glad to finish my errands.

This year the adults had drawn names for a gift exchange, so there would be only one gift to buy per adult. Although we didn't limit the number of gifts for the kids, Maria and I decided to do what we did last year and buy just one gift for each other's children. We would also exchange a couple's gift for each other too. Thankfully, by the end of the day, I had everything wrapped and ready.

That night, Nica and Angela joined us for a sleepover. They popped corn and strung long lines of it around the tree. "Mama and Mike, come look!"

The girls were grinning. "Wow," Mike said. "You've done a great job. It's pretty."

"That's so unusual to do it the way you have. It's beautiful," I added in awe.

"It was Nica's idea to tie the ribbons onto it," Isabella said.

It was fun to see Nica's creativity coming out. She had begun to paint in different mediums, and with colorful swishes of her brush, she was turning out some fascinating work. I was hoping that her artwork could win her a college scholarship.

Angela was coming into her own as well. She had shot up in height and was now as tall as Isabella. Angela was into fashion, carefully choosing each outfit and highlighting her outfits with accessories. She had plans to own a boutique someday.

Isabella and Sammy had already announced that they would use their psychic abilities to help find missing children and protect them from human trafficking. They already did that with Roberto, the Las Vegas Chief of Police.

The girls and Sammy were still young, and time would add its own twists to each of their journeys. But looking at them now, I had a strong sense that with the proper guidance, each would succeed.

I was getting sleepy. We'd already eaten, and I'd cleaned the kitchen with Mike's help. The girls were glued to the television in the living room, watching a hallmark-like movie, "A Christmas Kiss." They were at the age where they liked watching romance movies, becoming increasingly aware of how the ladies dressed and what type of makeup they wore. I could hear them chattering in the background.

Mike came up behind me and put his arms around me. "Sweetheart, you look beat. Why don't you go to bed? I'll meet Romano, Randy, Cal, and Virginia at the hotel. They'll understand if you're not there. I'm sure they're tired too."

"That sounds great," I said as I wiggled around to face him and kissed his waiting lips.

"Good. I'll check on the girls when I get back. I shouldn't be long."

I went to kiss the girls goodnight. They halted the movie. "Mama? Are you okay?"

I bit back a smile. Isabella acted like an overly protective nurse fussing at my pregnancy. "Just tired, sweetie. I'm heading to bed. Mike will check in with you when he returns."

I barely remembered Mike coming to bed. After the first few hours of a deep sleep, I slept fitfully. It was almost a relief to see daylight peeking in through the shutters. I snuggled against Mike, glad for his warmth. He automatically wrapped his arms around me, holding me tight. "It's too early to get up," he moaned.

"I know. I'm sorry, but I couldn't get back to sleep."

"Here, let me massage your back."

The baby protested as I rolled away from him to get more onto my stomach. I placed Mike's hand on my belly, and we chuckled at his constant kicking. I rolled back and once again moved my body against Mike's. It was a tender moment.

"I love you, Rosie. I'm going to love our son, too," he whispered into my ear.

My eyes watered. How did I get so lucky?

I heard the girls giggling in Isabella's bedroom, excited about what the day would bring. After showering and getting dressed, I searched for a cup of coffee. Mike was in the kitchen, and I eagerly reached for the mug of coffee he held out to me. Just then, we heard Cal, Virginia, Romano, and Randy at the front door. Mike and I headed there and opened it to see them brushing off the light snow covering them and their bags of presents. It was Romano's and Randy's second visit to the house here in Santa Fe, so once inside, it was no surprise that Romano immediately went into the kitchen to check out the food. Randy caught my eye and winked at me. A few minutes later, Romano entered the living room with an apron wrapped around his growing belly. "It's time for breakfast. Who wants what?"

"Pancakes!" the girls screamed.

"Blueberry pancakes?" Romano asked.

"Yes, please!" shouted Isabella.

He grinned broadly and puffed up his chest with pleasure at their eagerness. Soon, all of us were standing around him, waiting our turn for his pancakes. Virginia stood next to him, buttering and pouring syrup over the cakes and adding crisp bacon strips before she handed the plate to the next person in line. I held out plastic cups of cut-up fresh fruit, which completed our simple brunch and coffee, tea, and hot cocoa.

Soon came Karen, Coyote, Grandmother, and Angel. It was exactly a year ago that Angel's son (Nica's brother and Grandmother's grandson) had been murdered. Coyote and Karen were the ones who'd found him. I was keenly aware that all of them were trying to keep that memory at bay and remain focused on the new baby coming into their lives. We greeted them with hugs and kisses and a hardy "Ho, Ho, Ho" from Romano, patting his belly, pretending to be Santa. We laughed at his antics, and I moved everyone inside the house after I greeted them with a kiss.

When I came to stand before Grandmother, she took my arm and led me away from the others. "How are you, my daughter? Things are well between you and Mike?"

"We couldn't be happier, Grandmother—my mother."

"Then, I'm at rest."

I thought her statement was a bit odd. "Are you looking forward to becoming a great-grandmother?"

"Yes, soon," she said with a nod. "A Christmas bundle, I think."

I looked deep into her eyes. "I think you're right about that. I've felt it too." I kissed her weathered cheeks. "I love you so much, Grandmother. Thank you for being here."

Next came Maria and her family. Angela stepped forward to take the baby from Maria. Rosa was now a fast-traveling toddler, getting into everything. When Rosa saw me, she held her arms wide, calling "Wosie."

Hearing her say my name, I reached out for her. "Hi, little girl, whom I love so much. How are you?"

Looking past me, she began to squirm in my arms. "Down," she demanded.

I placed her on the floor and watched as she ran on sturdy legs into the kitchen area, where I had a cloth doll waiting for her. She grabbed the doll by the hair, turned around with a smile, and declared ownership. "Mine!"

We laughed. It was clear that, with three older brothers, she had to claim what she considered hers, or else she'd lose out. The three boys stood near the front door, gathered around Miguel, who had his hands full of casseroles and other food packages. Maria and I stepped forward to lighten his load. With a nod from their dad, the three boys raced inside and headed to the kitchen area, where I'd made space for them to play the computer games I'd laid out. I couldn't believe the difference a year made when I looked at them and realized how much they'd grown.

They were as close as brothers could be. At eight, Armando was the oldest and the tallest, lean like his father. Next came Riccardo, who, at age 6, was round like his mother and most likely wouldn't be as tall as his brothers. Little Miguel was almost four and was handsome like his brothers but with a more cheerful demeanor. It was fun to see them with their heads together, figuring out how one of the computer games worked. With all of their energy, Maria had her hands full.

Angela was in charge of her little sister today. Interestingly, with Karen's baby and mine on the way, Isabella and Nica were testing out the responsibility of being the "big sister" by helping Angela with Rosa. The girls took off into Isabella's bedroom with Rosa.

The guys grabbed Mexican beer and went into the living room to watch another football game while we women gathered in the dining room. Karen sat in a chair across from me at the table, and it was apparent she was uncomfortable. She began to fidget in her seat, trying to get comfortable. Acknowledging my unspoken question if she was okay, she gave me a thumbs up. "Just the normal discomfort," she said.

After cleaning up and things were settling down, Karen, always the curious teacher, lumbered her way back into the kitchen area to check on the boys' progress on the computer games they were playing. A few minutes later, we heard shrieks of laughter. I went to see what was happening, and as I rounded the corner, the three boys were giggling and pointing at Karen. There Karen stood, looking puzzled as she stared at the puddle at her feet. Her water had broken.

"Auntie Karen went pee-pee all over herself," laughed Riccardo.

Maria was close behind me, and her eyes widened at the sight before us. "Oh, Karen, your water broke!"

Maria and I looked at each other excitedly while Karen stood panicked and excited with her expressions, taking turns crossing her face.

I called out to everyone, "Sarah's on her way!"

We packed Karen into the front of the car while I clambered into the back, and we took off, excited to bring a new baby into the world.

***

Amazingly, Karen's labor went smoothly for a first-time birth, and 12 hours later, on a beautiful early Christmas morning, Sarah came into the world with a red face, topped by a mop of dark hair and squalling. As soon as her father picked her up, she became quiet, entranced with his musical voice hushing her. He looked at the home midwife and me with teary dark eyes that overflowed as he held the baby high into the air and said something in Tewa, the old Indian language. Then, he bent low to kiss Karen, speaking the same language. She smiled and said something back to him in Tewa. It was an intimate moment that made me turn away in embarrassment, leaving them alone at this personal time.

As soon as I'd texted Mike that Sarah had arrived, he'd headed out to pick me up to return home. When Mike came, Coyote went outside and pulled him in. Mike smiled at me as he followed Coyote into the bedroom where the new baby was lying. Her eyes were open, looking around, probably trying to figure out what'd happened to her, I thought with a smile. My heart expanded when I saw Mike carefully hold his finger to touch the baby's tiny hand. He looked almost as proud of her as Coyote did. "She's so little!"

We laughed. I walked to Karen's side. She opened her eyes and reached for my hand. "I can make your wedding now. I was worried I wouldn't be able to."

"Yes, and Nancy and Susannah will get to meet Sarah!"

We smiled at each other. I kissed Karen's cheek. "Get some sleep, and I'll call you later, okay?"

She nodded and was instantly asleep.

# CHAPTER 5

I t seemed like it was time to get up by the time I got to bed. Christmas morning began with Isabella and Sweet Pea jumping onto the bed. "Get up, Mama!"

Mike had gotten up a few minutes earlier to get the coffee started. Soon, just Cal, Virginia, Romano, and Randy would join us here. Coyote, Karen, Nica, Angel, and Grandmother would spend their holiday at the Pueblo. Maria and her family were at home for the mad circus time Christmas brought them.

After they arrived, we opened our presents and spent the rest of the day relaxing. There was a football game to watch, and I took a nap while Isabella spent time with Cal and Virginia. Romano and Randy had chef friends in two different restaurants in Santa Fe, and they went off to visit them. One of them had asked if Romano would be willing to be a guest chef the following night at his place. As soon as we heard he would do that, we made reservations at the restaurant to support him.

Cal and Virginia were leaving the next day to visit friends in Albuquerque. They'd return by the 30th, the day that Mike and I were to be married. It would be a small wedding with just the family—the same people who were with us on Christmas Eve, plus baby Sarah, Brian (Mike's business partner), my other sister-friends, Nancy and Susannah, and their partners.

I looked forward to legalizing Mike's and my relationship because it'd give Isabella the security she needed. Mike adored her, and they had a close relationship despite her resistance to calling him Dad. Mike didn't seem upset by that and willingly referred to her as his daughter when asked. Her uncle, Miguel, had come a long way in accepting that his niece was my "daughter" and now Mike's. Slowly, he won Isabella's heart due to his acceptance of the situation. She'd begun to show him some of the affection that'd been missing, and Miguel was a smart enough man to be grateful.

***

After Isabella was tucked into bed with Sweet Pea the night before our wedding and Brian snored in the guest room, I snuggled against Mike. I was happy that I'd be sleeping with Mike as my husband after tomorrow. I fell into a dream state —that in-between time of sleeping/not sleeping—and Tom Little Horse came to me in a dream. He wore a crooked smile on his handsome face. "Be happy, Little Bird. Know that I'll always love you. I wish you well."

I awoke with a sense of relief. My eyelids were matted with drying tears. Tom's coming to me had set me free to love Mike with no regrets, and I was grateful. Sensing my unrest, Mike pulled me tight against him. "Hush, sweetheart, all is well."

It was a simple but beautiful wedding with all our family and friends surrounding us. We had tied our rings on a ribbon around Sweet Pea's neck, and she sat between Isabella and Brian, standing by our sides as we said our vows. When it came time to exchange rings, it soon became evident that Brian had nervously tied the ribbon too tightly. We all chuckled as he bent beside Isabella and struggled with the knot. Soon enough, the rings and vows were exchanged, and the Chief pronounced us man and wife.

Afterward, we sister-friends took turns holding Sarah, oohing and ahhing over her perfection. We brushed away our tears, acknowledging Karen's happiness, something we had wanted for her for a long time.

As we huddled around the baby, Nancy's eyes sparkled. "I probably shouldn't say anything until the doctor confirms it, but I'm pretty sure I'm pregnant."

I whooped. "That's wonderful, Nancy! How far along are you?"

"Just a few weeks. But I won't relax until the doctor tells me I'm pregnant. I'll let you all know as soon as I find out." She and Steve were going through in vitro fertilization; her pregnancy was fantastic news.

We hugged in a group. Although Susannah and Henry had agreed they'd have no children because of their abusive upbringings, a wistful expression crossed Susannah's face. I wondered if she felt left out with the two of us pregnant and Karen with her new baby. I turned to her and whispered, "Are you okay, Susannah?"

She kissed my cheek. "Not to worry. It was just a moment that passed. You understand?"

"I do, my dear friend."

Mike pulled me to his side. "The hotel wants to know if you're ready for them to serve dinner."

I pulled his arm close to me to see the time on his watch. "Golly, it's getting late. Tell them yes, and I'll get people to sit down."

Mike and I sat in the center of the small head table with Isabella on one side and Brian on the other. Someone clicked glasses together. "Kiss, kiss, kiss."

I laughed and twisted my head to reach Mike's lips. He smiled at me. "I love you, my queen. Thank you for marrying me."

"I'm happy to oblige," I said with a wink.

"Speech, speech."

Mike stood up and remained quiet momentarily, drawing everyone's attention. Then he began ...

"The first time I saw Rosie, she was the most beautiful girl I'd ever seen. I thought Brian was joking when he wanted me to pretend to be Rosie's boyfriend—and get paid for doing it!" People chuckled. "She kept me on my toes. As her security guard, I soon discovered she was always getting herself into trouble, which we've all learned is not unusual for her." Everyone laughed.

He became still and thoughtful. "I didn't think I stood a chance with her, and she didn't seem interested in me at all," he said, smiling at me. "It was when I saw Rosie with Isabella that I knew I wanted to be a part of her life ... part of her family. I also wanted the same love Rosie has for Isabella to be mine. There is such a strong bond between them, and now sharing their love with me after what we've been through has made me the happiest man alive. And today, besides a wife and daughter, I'll soon have a son." Unabashedly, he wiped tears away. A few others did the same. "How lucky can a guy get?"

Mike looked across the room. "This wouldn't be possible without Maria and Miguel. I toast both of you for loving Isabella enough to share her with us. Thank you for allowing us to become one big family. Here, here," he announced, lifting his glass in a toast.

Maria beamed, and Miguel's face reddened as attention was drawn to him. But he raised his glass in acknowledgment and quickly nodded appreciation. I smiled at them. Yes, Miguel had come a long way in accepting things as they were with Isabella, and it was beautiful for all involved.

Mike stooped and kissed me thoroughly on the lips.

"Here, here! Congratulations to the bride and groom!" called out Brian.

I looked around at everyone sitting at the tables, helping to celebrate and honor Mike and me as a couple. I couldn't believe how fortunate I was. I felt a cool breeze across the back of my neck and smiled. "Hi, Gram," I whispered to her spirit.

"Hi, darling girl. I'm so happy for you." She sent me a vision of red roses for love.

"Love you too, Gram," I whispered.

***

As we packed to leave Santa Fe, it was with the understanding that I probably wouldn't be back until after the baby was born in the spring. Isabella was old enough to fly by herself, so she'd return for spring vacation to spend time with her sister-friends and family.

31

I was torn. I was sad to leave Santa Fe but excited to know I'd have my son with me the next time I returned.

# CHAPTER 6

T he months flew by. My pregnancy had gone well so far. But that night, I woke up in pain and foreboding. My lower back was killing me. I turned onto my side, and the ache lessened. What had I done to my back? I wondered. I closed my eyes and tried to get back to sleep. My stomach rumbled, and I felt what I thought must be gas pains. What had I eaten? I flopped onto my back again and bent my legs to ease the pain. That didn't help. I turned onto my side again. Nothing seemed to make a difference.

Mike flipped over and mumbled, 'You okay?"

"Yeah, sorry. Something I ate isn't agreeing with me. Go back to sleep."

He turned away and was soon snoring again.

An acid taste rose in my throat. I swallowed it and grabbed for the water I kept at my bedside. My heart began to pound. The baby wasn't due for two weeks, and I hadn't read anywhere that part of labor was a sick stomach. I intuitively knew my discomfort wasn't because of something I'd eaten, and what I was experiencing wasn't normal labor. When an increasing pain sliced through the right side of my body, I knew something was up. I shook Mike.

"Mike, wake up. You've got to call the doctor. Something isn't right."

"Are you in labor?" he asked nervously.

"I think it's more than that. Something's wrong. We need to go to the hospital right now."

"What are we going to do about Isabella?"

"I'll call Virginia. Come on, hurry."

When we got to the hospital, the nurse began questioning whether I was in labor. I wanted to scream with frustration. I had a vision of the baby not able to breathe. I rose from my wheelchair and lurched down the hallway, searching for my doctor … any doctor.

"The baby can't breathe. Please do something," I yelled.

My doctor was hurrying down the hallway toward me. He ordered the nurse, who'd heard us and had come to help, to lay me on the gurney so he could check my vital signs. Mike came to my side with his face drained of color. He was frightened and grabbed the doctor's arm. "Help her. If she says the baby can't breathe, she knows. She's psychic. Do whatever she says—please listen to her!"

The doctor turned from Mike to monitor the baby's heartbeat. "The baby is in distress. Let's get her into the emergency room right now."

The woman from behind the admittance desk approached. "You'll need to sign some papers before she can be admitted."

34

Both Mike and the doctor looked at the woman in astonishment. The doctor turned to her. "Get the hell out of the way."

Mike took hold of my hand and ran down the hallway beside the gurney until we reached the operating room.

"You'll have to stay outside," ordered the doctor.

"No! I'm not leaving her!"

"See the stairs there? Climb up them. It's an operating theatre. You can watch the whole thing from there."

"It's alright, Mike, I'll be fine. I love you."

He kissed me hurriedly. "I love you too, Rosie."

I heard the shuffling of feet and muffled urgent voices echoing in the operating room all around me. Then, I felt a prick that narrowed my light and put me into a closing world of darkness. I barely had enough time to whisper, "Please, God, let the baby be okay."

The darkness became complete, and after quite some time, I felt myself floating, unattached. Everything slowed as I entered a tunnel and saw a light far, far away. I became intrigued by its brightness and its pull, drawing me closer. I began to run toward it in slow motion, feeling freer the closer I got to the light. With every step, the light expanded. It seemed to take forever for me to reach it, and when I did, people were gathered there as if they were waiting for me. I recognized my mother and father and even my grandmother. Why were they there? I was so happy to see them that I began to cry. They didn't move toward me, only shook their head, not wanting me there. Then Tom Little Horse stepped forward. He held his arms out to me, and I ran into them.

"What are you doing here? You're not supposed to be here," he said.

"I'm not?" I asked, confused.

"No, our son needs you to help him grow into a man. You need to go back."

I began to cry again. "But it's so beautiful here."

"It's not your time. You're needed back there. I love you, Little Bird. I'll be here waiting for you when it's your turn to join us. Now go!" he urged, clapping his hands together, making a loud sound.

At the sound of his clapping, all began to fade away, and I felt myself falling. Soon, muffled sounds became clear. "She's waking up, doctor."

"Bring her husband in so I can talk to both of them at the same time."

"Yes, doctor."

I groaned and tried to sit up. "Where's my baby?" I croaked, panicked.

A nurse was holding a bundle in her arms, rocking back and forth. When she heard me, she headed my way. "You have a beautiful little boy," she said, handing the baby to me.

I peeked inside and saw two dark eyes observing me. He wore a serious expression, and suddenly without reason, he smiled. "Oh, my beautiful boy," I said while looking him over. "You've got your daddy's eyes," I whispered in wonderment.

Mike came hurrying in, dressed in an operating gown and matching cap. When he saw that we were okay, he began to cry. I held the baby out for him to take.

"He's so beautiful," he murmured, peeking into the bundle. "My son." He smiled through more tears. "Thank you, my queen."

Remembering Tom Little Horse's words—our son—I remained silent. Being a father was more than a man's seed. It was all about how you treated someone and helped

36

him to maneuver through life. I knew Mike was this little boy's perfect father, so I said, "No, my love, thank you."

The doctor entered the room. "Congratulations on your beautiful boy. We were lucky to be able to get to him in time. However, we found a problem. When we opened you up, we discovered a large cyst on one of your ovaries that was still actively growing and infringing on the sac, causing stress for the baby. Something we hadn't seen before. When the cyst burst, it caused major bleeding. We finally got the bleeding to stop once we completely removed the cyst. But the damage it caused may affect your chances of becoming pregnant again. We can only wait and hope for the best. I'm sorry not to be able to be more definite."

Mike and I looked at each other in dismay. No more children? My grandmother's spirit floated around me. "Enjoy those you have now, Rosie girl, for they will bring you much happiness."

"Thank you, doctor, for letting us know," I said, saddened by the realization that I may not produce a child for Mike with his own bloodline.

"Right now, I think we have our hands full with this little guy," Mike stated as he rubbed the baby's cheek with his finger. "He smiled!"

We all laughed. "Please don't tell my husband that's because he has gas," I said teasingly to the doctor.

"I heard that. No, it was a real smile," Mike insisted. "Look!"

And right on cue, our little boy smiled.

Later, Isabella entered my hospital room and raced to where Mike sat in the chair, holding the baby in his arms. He held the baby out to her, and she gathered him into her arms, peeking inside the blanket that swaddled him. "Oh,

Mama and Mike, he's so cute! What are we going to name him?" she asked, turning to me with a questioning look.

"One of the names we discussed was Jack. It means God is Gracious, and I think the name fits after his narrow escape from death. What do you think, Mike?"

"I think Jack is the perfect name for him," Mike said. "It suits the little guy."

"I think so, too," said Isabella, smiling at the tiny face studying her earnestly.

As he grew older, even the sound of his name seemed to fit him—sure and powerful.

# CHAPTER 7

T he next few years flew by, with Jack learning to walk and talk. One day, when he was four years old, I stood unnoticed in his bedroom doorway and watched as he crouched before his old toy box and laughingly pulled out a stuffed horse. He held it up in the air. "Yes, I like horses too. See, this is my favorite one! I used to pretend it was real."

I stepped into the room. "Who are you talking to, Jack?"

"My father," he answered quickly.

"Mike isn't here, Jack," I stated, looking around.

"I know. I'm talking to my heaven father."

"Ooh. Does he visit you often?"

"Uh-huh. But he came to tell me he would be gone for a while. He said he loves me, and you, too, Mama. He said that I'm to be good to my earth father. He's going to be watching over all of us."

I bent down and kissed Jack on top of the head. "That's nice to know, isn't it?"

He smiled. "Yup."

"Are you ready to go downstairs? Dinner is almost ready. Daddy is grilling hamburgers with Grandfather, your favorite thing to eat."

"Yea!" Jack ran out the door and pounded down the stairs.

I looked up to the heavens. "So, Gram, it looks like we have another psychic in the family, doesn't it?"

*"Yes, my darling girl. I'm afraid it does,"* she laughed.

I picked up the stuffed horse and put him back into the toy box. I whispered, "I love you too, Tom," as my hand enclosed the solitaire diamond I wore around my neck. It was from the engagement ring Tom had bought to give to me before he was killed. At the urging of his housekeeper, I wore it to honor the man I'd once loved. I'd never told anyone where the diamond had come from, and there was no need to do otherwise. Mike probably wouldn't care, but I didn't want to make an issue of it and take anything away from my love for Mike, who had my heart.

Isabella was downstairs with Sammy, who was joining us for dinner. He stood next to Isabella, holding Sweet Pea in his arms. Now nearly 18 years old, each of them had become even more stunning in looks—Isabella with her slim figure and all the right curves, smooth Mexican complexion, dark eyes, dark curly hair, and a ready smile. Sammy was the opposite with his near-white hair, bright eyes (one blue and one green), chiseled features in a ruddy complexion, and muscular frame. As a child, he had been beautiful; as a man, he was stunning. He'd outgrown his stutter, and his confidence was evident in his movements and words.

He and Isabella were inseparable and had already announced they would be life partners. No one doubted that after seeing them together. When I periodically read the Tarot cards for them, their future together looked bright.

Isabella and Sammy's psychic abilities were more significant than mine, and they'd had a working relationship with the Chief of Police for years now. This past week, they'd been asked to participate in a study regarding intuition, empathy, and psychic abilities here in Las Vegas. They'd gotten permission from the Wilson Charter School to go on sabbatical for the four months it'd take to complete that study. As part of it, one weekend each month, they would attend classes at the School of Metaphysics in Arizona, where I'd attended. It was my turn to take them in a few days, and I was looking forward to being there, particularly since I would be allowed to sit in the classroom.

"Hey, Sammy! Look what I made!" hollered Jack, holding up a crayon drawing of a creature resembling one of the Star Wars characters.

After setting Sweet Pea down, Sammy reached for the paper that Jack held out and asked, "What's this?"

"Someone from outer space."

"Really? He's pretty ugly," chuckled Sammy.

"But he's really nice," Jack implored.

"Let me see," said Isabella. One look at the drawing, and Isabella ruffled Jack's hair. "That's pretty cool. I think you're a good artist. Show it to Mike." Isabella still called Mike by his name and not Daddy as Jack did.

"Daddy! Want to see this?" hollered Jack.

"Sure, buddy, bring it here," he commanded, "Grandfather can see it too."

"Okay," he said, running to where they were grilling outside.

I smiled as I watched Mike bend down to study the drawing. "It's pretty cool. What planet is this guy from?"

"Mars," he answered with a giggle.

Mike turned to Grandfather. "We went to the library and found a book about planets and stars. Jack and I have been studying it."

I winked at Virginia, sitting in the great room, listening and watching everything happening. I joined her and refilled her glass of chardonnay. "Are you sure you don't mind watching Jack while Mike and I are away?"

"Heavens, no. Cal and I love to have him with us."

"I'll be in Arizona with the kids, and Mike is returning to the Boston office for a few days to work on a project with Brian."

Virginia shook her head in disgust. "I'm so glad that Allison girl is no longer with their company. She was nothing but trouble."

"Brian had to put his foot down when she began to fawn over every male client. It was long past time for her to be let go, anyway. Hopefully, she'll seek professional help to straighten out her constant need for attention and praise."

"Hamburgers are done, everyone! Come and get them!" shouted Mike. Watching Jack trying to reach for one, Mike said, "Jack, let Mama help you."

Jack loved food, and it was a joy to see him eat. But, at the same time, he needed to learn to wait his turn. "Let Virginia and Isabella get their hamburgers first," I said.

He smiled at me. "Okay, Mama. Then, I'm next, right?"

"Yup, then you're next," I agreed.

We all sat at the large dining room table to eat. When I looked around at those sitting there, I held back tears. I felt so blessed to have them in my life despite a deep ache that it seemed likely that Mike and I wouldn't be adding any more children to the table. The next little one would probably belong to Isabella and Sammy. The Tarot cards seemed to confirm that idea.

When Friday came, I drove Mike to the airport to catch his flight to Boston. He grabbed and kissed my hand as we pulled into the departure area. "I'm going to miss you, Rosie, even though I won't be gone that long."

"I'm going to miss you more, handsome. We're long overdue for another weekend away to spend time together alone. What do you say?"

"I like the way you think. I'm ready. Why don't you call Romano and Randy to get the number for that place they're always bragging about? That place we went to a few years ago."

"Yes, that'd be perfect. Please call me when you arrive, okay? I want to make sure you get there safe and sound. Is Brian picking you up?"

"Yup. I'll get to meet his new girlfriend, too."

"I can't wait to hear what you think about this one compared to all the others. Brian said she wasn't his usual type of woman, so let's hope this one is right for him."

"You can't stand to see him unsettled, can you?"

I chuckled. "That's true. I want Brian happy, and I don't think he will be happy until he finds the right woman and begins to make some babies. At least that's what he told me the last time he was here."

"Well, I'll let you know. Meantime, lean over my way so that I can kiss you goodbye."

I smiled and moved toward him. After a long, romantic kiss, a car horn behind us beeped several times, impatient to get our attention to move along. Mike unloaded himself and his bag, and I pulled away. It was time to pick up Sammy and Isabella to head to Arizona. My heart beat happily at the thought of what lay ahead for the three of us. I couldn't wait to be back at my old school again.

# CHAPTER 8

**A**s we drove closer to Phoenix, Arizona, I became uneasy with the feeling that we should turn around and go back home. I looked in the rear-view mirror to see Sammy slumped against the seat with his eyes closed, snoozing. Sensing my anxiety, Isabella asked me, "What is it, Mama?"

"I don't know. I feel uneasy. Do you sense something?"

"I'm hoping that what I've been feeling for the past few hours is excitement about what we're going to learn today."

Understanding that the Universe often keeps us from knowing everything before an event happens so our journey wouldn't be disturbed, I mumbled, "From your lips to God's ears."

When I pulled into the underground parking garage, my heart began to pound, and Sammy seemed on edge, looking out the back window, frowning. 'I don't think that we should park here, Rosie. Can you pull around and get us out of here?"

I stopped the car and put it in reverse. As I did, two young men who'd raced from between the parked cars to get to us were thumping on the side car windows. With one on each side of the vehicle, they pounded on the windows and yelled for us to get out.

"Don't stop, Rosie. Back up!" yelled Sammy.

I stepped on the gas, and the car roared back in reverse toward the gatekeeper's booth where we'd entered. The guard stepped out of the booth to see what the fuss was about. Then, the two men came forward, one holding a gun. The guard flapped his hands at them and yelled, "Go on! Get outta here!"

"Oh, yeah? Who's going to make us? You?"

As we continued to back away, it exposed the guard before us, an easy mark for the two young men. I yelled, "Get out of the way!" to the guard and raced the car toward the two men, surprising them as I hollered, "Hold on, Isabella and Sammy!"

The car nicked each of the guys, spreading them across the hood of the car for a few seconds before they fell to the ground. The noise from their bodies hitting the car and then hitting the pavement resounded throughout the garage. It was a sickening sound, reminding me of my car accident several years earlier. I immediately stomped down on the break, stalling the car. I held the steering wheel with shaking hands, bowing my head onto them. Isabella was already on her cell phone talking to the police. As soon as I stopped the car, Sammy leaped from it and ran to kick away the gun that had fallen from the groaning men. With all his experience working with the police, he knew enough not to touch it and leave his fingerprints.

The guard ran forward and held his gun over the two men. "One move, and I'll shoot the two of you, you thieving bastards."

Sirens became louder, and two police cars and an ambulance entered the garage and pulled over beside our stalled car. The older policeman came to where I was still sitting behind the wheel. "Are you alright, miss?"

I nodded numbly. "I will be as soon as you put these men behind bars."

"Over here," yelled the policeman to the medic. "Check her out, will you? I think she may be in shock," he said as I began to shiver all over.

We gave our statements to the police and told them where they could find us if they needed more information. Although the car's front end was dented, I could still drive it without problems. So once the area was cleared, I drove out of the garage near the school in Phoenix's poor section. I headed to the luxury hotel in the city's center, where I'd made reservations for us to stay for two nights.

I tried not to have my dark thoughts about the incident at the garage take away any enthusiasm from Isabella and Sammy to attend the class, which would begin in two hours. After settling in our suite with a separate room and bath for Sammy, we went to the hotel's café for lunch. Although still shaken up by the experience in the parking garage, we enthusiastically placed our orders. Then, I turned to Isabella and Sammy with a smile. "That was quite a welcome to Phoenix. A lot has changed since I went to school here."

"Why do bad things have to happen, Mama? I don't know what I'm to learn from this."

"You can't have peaks without valleys. I know that sounds much simpler than it is, but …."

"I'm just glad the guard wasn't killed," interrupted Sammy.

"Me, too," I said. "Let's keep this among ourselves until we return home safe and sound. I don't want Mike to worry about us; he has enough on his mind."

Isabella chuckled. "You mean you don't want to hear Mike say you're always getting into trouble."

I laughed. "And that, too, smarty pants."

Sammy studied us as Isabella, and I laughed together. "You two have such a special bond," he stated.

I smiled at Isabella and patted her hand. "Yes, we do, and it's wonderful! I looked at my watch. "It's time to call for an Uber to take us to the school. Do you have everything you need to take with you?"

They both nodded, and I called for the check.

# CHAPTER 9

L oading into the Uber car, I became excited to attend the class at the school. Arriving there brought back memories. It was the first time I'd formally addressed the idea that I could use my psychic gifts to help others. When I had the Tarot cards in front of me, their meanings became nothing more than an avenue for my mind to escape to where I *knew* what was going to happen or what had already taken place in the past. In that space, there was no definition of time. No tomorrow, no yesterday—only space.

And, of course, there were times when my uncertainty reared its ugly head, and I could only guess. But all in all, I'd learned to control what I said to others to remain within the boundaries of discernment. Lately, I had too often pushed away specific warnings and feelings to have the freedom to live my own life. The only bad thing about that was I needed to protect those who were my responsibility. So, to say that I was looking forward to spending more time in a classroom with other intuitive, psychic people was an understatement. I hoped to gain a better insight into how to handle Jack's newly discovered abilities.

When we stepped into the assigned classroom, I was delighted to see my former teacher, who beamed at seeing me. "Rosalie? Rosalie Bennett? I can't believe you're here. Come on in! And who are these two beautiful people with you?"

"This is Isabella, my daughter, and her best friend, Sammy Brooks."

"Mack Carson," he said as he shook hands with Isabella and Sammy. He turned to me, holding his arm wide and hugging me. "Nice to have you back, Rosie."

"Thank you, Mack."

There were only 12 of us in the class that day. To "test" us out, he called one of the older students up front and called on Sammy to tell the rest of the class what he "sensed" about the person. I watched as Mack's eyes widened at all that Sammy "saw" about the person. Then, he turned to Isabella. "What else do you sense about this person, Isabella?"

"It's pretty personal. I'm not sure I should say anything."

The girl standing up front nodded, "It's okay. There are no secrets here. Go ahead."

"You just purchased a pair of fancy red bikini pants and matching bra from Victoria's Secret, hoping that Thomas will want to make love tonight."

The girl blushed a bright red.

Seeing her red face, Isabella mumbled, "Sorry."

The girl giggled at being caught out. "No, no. That's okay. It's true enough."

Everyone turned in their seat and stared at the boy in the back. "That's kinda what I had in mind, too," Thomas said with pink cheeks.

The class broke into laughter.

"As you can see, there are very few secrets here," Mack said with a chuckle.

It was interesting when it came time for Isabella to take her turn up front. The others saw her as a little Indian girl and me as her sister back then and now as her mother. It was probably easy for them to see that because we readily acknowledged our relationship. But even more interesting was one who saw Isabella in the future with a circle of women around her. Men tried to get to Isabella, but the women held them back. A prophetic vision.

I thought I understood that vision, mainly because she was helping me with an aspect of Cal's having set up a Trust in his mother's name to help women off the streets. I was in the process of buying two houses to be used as safe houses—one in Las Vegas and one in Santa Fe. Although we hadn't discussed it yet, I hoped Isabella would help me run it.

Sammy's turn up front showed him to be married to Isabella and several children in their life. One saw him wearing a holster with a gun on his waist. I chuckled to myself when I heard that. I knew he wanted to work with Mike as a detective, but he hadn't built up the nerve to ask him yet. I wondered if his parents, Maggie and David, would be upset that he wouldn't be a lawyer like his father. Time will tell. But again, his parents seemed to always roll with whatever their only child wanted that was within reason.

I refused when invited up front, and Mack let me get away with it. However, I readily agreed to do the testing

I remembered from the past to assess our intuition and abilities. I wondered if my capabilities had expanded with time or had withered some from my concerted effort to push away from them.

We paired up, half of us going into the empty room across the hall and spreading out—the same for those who stayed behind. Two large boxes next to Mack's desk were filled with different items. We were asked to pick five items and place them in front of us. Then we had to hold up one thing and concentrate on it for three minutes. There was a buzzer that timed us. Our partner in the other room had to write down what they saw.

When we joined together, it was amazing at the accuracy of the item held up and what the other person saw. We switched places and ended up with nearly the same results. I missed one and realized how little I did with my Tarot cards now compared to my past. Maybe it was time to get back to them again.

The weekend flew by, and it was time to head home. My head was spinning from all the higher energy work we'd done. Isabella and Sammy were enthralled with what they had learned and kept "talking" to each other mentally, testing their accuracy. They were unbelievable together.

As we raced down the road, all three of us said at the same time, "Accident ahead." We smiled at each other and our newfound awareness. We took a bypass to avoid the accident and headed home without any other issues.

Now that we were away from Phoenix, I let my mind wander back to the incident in the garage. In a split second, without thought, I'd overcome my fear and dared to block those men from hurting the guard. Yet, at the same time, hadn't I endangered Isabella and Sammy? Choices …

always choices without the sure knowledge of the results. What a rollercoaster life is! I thought.

# CHAPTER 10

A s we approached Las Vegas, Isabella and Sammy received a text message from Roberto asking if they could stop by the police station to talk about a person who'd been newly reported missing.

"Mama, come with us. We can stop there before we head home. It won't take that long."

We pulled into the station and went inside. It was abuzz with people rushing about. Roberto smiled when he saw me. "I'm glad to see you, Rosie. Thanks for coming."

Sammy and Isabella ran ahead into an office where a policeman was hovering over a computer, searching through it.

"What's going on?" I asked.

"C'mon in, and I'll explain."

We joined the others. "What's the scoop?" asked Sammy.

Roberto said, "A few hours ago, we received a frantic phone call from a woman in housekeeping at the Bellagio casino downtown. One of the guests there had hired her to babysit her daughter while she went downstairs to attend a show. The babysitter said she was gone for just a few minutes to use one of the bathrooms in the suite, and when she came back out, the door to the suite was wide open, and the little girl was gone."

"How old is the little girl?" asked Isabella.

"Eight years old."

I turned to Isabella, who looked at me with raised eyebrows. Worry crossed her face. She knew too well what could happen to eight-year-old girls kidnapped for sex.

A noise out front caught our attention. I turned to see Mike walk through the door. He looked surprised to see us there.

"Hey there, I wasn't expecting to see you here."

"I could say the same about you. When did you get in?" I asked.

"Just now," he replied. "I came right here."

I stepped closer to Mike to kiss him. He gave me a hurried peck, and eager to get on with the hunt, he asked, "What's going on?"

"Glad you made it, Mike. Let's you and I head to the casino to meet with the security guards to check out the security tape. I asked Isabella and Sammy to come here to see if they could receive any visions of where the girl might be. Jose, show them the pictures of the little girl sent to us online. I'll fill you in on the way, Mike."

The two rushed out, and I went to stand behind the officer sitting at the computer. The pictures of the little girl showed a beautiful blond-haired, blue-eyed girl who was adorable. Her heavy makeup and grown-up clothes took away from her youthful beauty. Goosebumps flashed across me, and I shivered. I never liked the idea of young girls dressing up like older sexy female models, competing for a title. It didn't seem right, but that type of thing was popular today. Indeed, though, not a good thing to do in a city like Las Vegas, where so many people go missing every day.

I closed my eyes and thought of the little girl. A vision flashed before me, and I saw her in a group with other children, but nothing more than that. I looked at Isabella and Sammy, who held hands with closed eyes. Suddenly, they came out of their trance-like state.

"I think I know where she is. Did you see what I saw?" Isabella asked Sammy.

"Yup," Sammy said. "Can you drive us to the Bellagio, Rosie?"

"Don't you think we should let Mike and Roberto know what you've seen?"

"We think she's hiding somewhere in the casino," Sammy said.

"We need to go there, Mama, and see for ourselves. Did you see anything?" asked Isabella.

"I saw her with a group of kids."

"That's what we saw, too," Isabella said.

Sammy nodded in agreement.

"Okay, let's go. Call Mike and Roberto and tell them we're on our way," I urged.

When we got there, I swung into the valet, and the three of us hopped out and went inside to meet with Roberto and Mike. A security guard was waiting for us and immediately led us into a secured section of offices hidden in the back of the casino. One of the rooms was filled with a dozen or more computers covering different casino areas where people went about their business unaware of being filmed.

We could hear Roberto and Mike in a separate room speaking with someone crying and upset. At first, I didn't know whether it was the housekeeper or the mother, but then we heard a raised voice demand hotly, "I want you to find my daughter now! She's got to be here somewhere! Where is that stupid woman who was supposed to be watching her? When this is done, I will sue the pants off all of you."

Roberto said, "We're doing all we can …."

"Obviously, not enough!" the woman bellowed.

"Remain calm. Thankfully, your daughter hasn't been gone that long," added Mike in a soothing tone. "We'll find her."

Roberto and Mike's relationship was unique. At certain times, Roberto called in Mike as an independent detective to help him find missing people. It was on a consultant basis, and the arrangement seemed to work out for them.

When we approached the room, Roberto saw us and asked desperately, "Anything?"

"We think she's here. Do you have a place where kids hang out? A game room or something?" Sammy asked.

"Yes, there's a game room off to the side of the movie theatre area. Do you think Elizabeth is there?" asked Roberto.

"We won't know without seeing it. If she isn't there, we still think she's in the casino somewhere," Sammy answered.

Isabella nodded in agreement.

Mike came out to join us. "She wants to talk to you, Roberto."

"Why don't you follow them to the game room to see if the girl is there? I'll see what the mother wants," suggested Roberto.

"I'll radio you and let you know as soon as we check it out. Come on, let's see what we can find," Mike said, turning to us. He put his arm around Sammy's shoulder. "Lead the way, kid."

Neither Isabella nor I reacted to Mike's evident attention to Sammy. Isabella and Sammy had been working with Mike for a while now, and it was understood that Sammy was hoping to join Mike's company after he finished school and attended the police academy. Isabella was okay with that. While Sammy was taking courses in criminology at UNLV, she was busy taking business classes there. I'd encouraged her to study business with the hope she'd be able to help me run the Trust for Cal to assist women caught up in drugs and working the streets to survive.

Isabella followed closely behind Mike and Sammy while I took the time to look around. I hadn't been to the Bellagio in a long time and wanted to see if I could find the vulnerable young girl who occasionally popped into my thoughts. Several years ago, I spotted her serving drinks as Mike, and I walked through the casino headed to one of the fantastic restaurants there. Mike took a picture of her on my phone, and every once in a while, I'd come upon it accidentally. Although that had been a terrible night for me, with Mike announcing he wasn't ready to move our relationship forward, I'd never forgotten the girl. If I ever saw her again, I promised myself that I'd make sure she was okay.

By the time I reached the game room, all three were standing in the center of the room, looking baffled. The space was empty.

# CHAPTER 11

"I can't believe there's nobody here!" Isabella said. "I was so sure she'd be here."

"Mike, do you know if the little girl beauty contest was here this past weekend?" I asked. "If so, are the contestants staying here too? Where are the other girls who competed? Maybe they'll know what happened to Elizabeth."

"Yes, she participated and won, according to her mother. I have no idea if the other girls are staying here too. I imagine so, but Roberto will know. Let's go back."

"Something isn't right," Sammy said, looking around. "Can we talk to the housekeeper?"

Mike radioed Roberto to ask if that could be arranged. Then, Mike listened intently and said, "Yeah, that's good you sent her back to their room in case Elizabeth shows up there. I'm glad you have a nurse to stay with her so she won't be alone. Yup, we're on our way back there now."

I sighed. "That poor woman. I can only imagine what Elizabeth's mother is going through."

We returned to the security offices to find the housekeeper seated in the room where the mother had been. A large glass window overlooked the hallway, and it was easy to see that the woman looked scared to death. I felt sorry for her.

We stood back out of the way as Mike went into the office and approached her. "Hello, madam, my name is Mike. I'm going to ask you some questions. Let's start from the beginning, shall we?"

She unconsciously pulled away from his towering figure standing over her but nodded gamely.

"What time did you arrive at the suite?"

"Around 6:30, and Elizabeth's mother left soon after.

"What were you and Elizabeth doing before you left to use the bathroom?"

"Elizabeth wanted to go downstairs to play a game, but her mother had said she couldn't leave the room. I told her that."

"Was she upset with you?"

"She called me names, ran into her bedroom, and slammed the door."

"Then what?" prodded Mike.

The housekeeper's face flushed a deep red. "By the time I was done in the bathroom and returned to the living room, the door was wide open, and she was gone."

Now things were falling into place, I thought.

"Do you have any idea where she might have gone?"

The housekeeper straightened her shoulders. "Her mother told me that Elizabeth was not allowed any sweets because she didn't want her to gain weight."

Isabella grabbed Sammy's arm. "Let's go. We've got this."

"What do you mean, Isabella?" I asked. "Do you know where she is?"

"Eating ice cream," Sammy answered with a smile.

"You two go ahead. I'll tell Mike and Roberto."

When Mike, Roberto, and I reached the food court, we saw Isabella and Sammy sitting at a table with other little girls in the competition. And right there, in the middle of it all, was Elizabeth stuffing her face with ice cream and holding up a half-eaten chocolate chip cookie. She was spooning the ice cream into her mouth so fast it was as if she was afraid someone would rip the food away from her.

When Elizabeth saw us, she shook her head. "No! I'm not going with you. I'm going to eat my ice cream."

"We'll wait," said Roberto.

One of the other girls looked between the men and Elizabeth. She asked, "Elizabeth, are they here for you?"

"Uh, huh. But I get to finish my ice cream first."

A woman sitting at the table rose and came toward us. "What's the problem, officer?"

"Are you one of the mothers here with the contest?" asked Roberto.

"Yes, my daughter is part of the group. Why?" she asked.

"Are you aware that Elizabeth ran away from her babysitter and had been missing? Her mother is frantic."

"Oh, my! I had no idea. Elizabeth told me that her mother said she could join us. I'm so sorry."

Just then, we heard a shriek. "There you are!" Fear crossed Elizabeth's face as she took in her mother's approaching figure. "And eating all that junk. How could you?"

Roberto held out his arm to waylay her. "I said she could finish up."

"Well, last time I checked, you aren't her mother," she snapped. "God, Elizabeth, you must never disobey me again, do you hear? Something bad could have happened to you."

A guilty expression flashed across Elizabeth's face and was soon replaced by a smile of success as she scraped the bottom of the dish to get out the last bit of the ice cream.

The woman who still stood by us turned to Elizabeth's mother. "I'm so sorry. I didn't know that Elizabeth didn't have your permission to be here. But at least she is safe, thank God. It could have been so much worse."

"I noticed you didn't stop her from eating ice cream," she scolded.

"Of course not. The girls deserve a little treat now and then," she retorted, annoyed.

"Ladies, ladies," said Mike. "Let's get this little girl back up to the suite, shall we?"

I waved to Isabella and Sammy that it was time for us to go. "I'll see you at home, handsome," I winked at Mike. "I see what you meant when you said Isabella and Sammy working with you has saved you time and worry."

He nodded. "See you at home in a bit."

After dropping Sammy off at his house, I drove home, and Isabella and I unloaded the car. Then I walked across our backyard into Cal and Virginia's property to pick up Jack.

When I got there, Jack was drawing at the kitchen table. I smiled at seeing him with his tongue caught in his teeth as he concentrated. He looked up and said, "Did you find her, Mama?"

"Who?" I asked.

"I closed my eyes and saw you looking for someone."

"Oh, yes, we did." I was amazed. His psychic abilities were growing, and I was dumbfounded that they were as strong as Isabella's and Sammy's.

Virginia handed me a glass of wine. "Thank you, and thanks so much for having Jack stay here my dear friend," I said.

"We've had a wonderful time, haven't we, Jack?"

In an earnest voice, he replied. "I always love coming here, Gramma."

"So, there you have it," I laughed as Virginia guided me into the living room.

"Come and tell me how your weekend went."

# CHAPTER 12

T he years flew by, with all of us busy. Jack was now nine years old, and Isabella had just turned 23. It was time to head to Santa Fe for the summer school break, and I was looking forward to being there, close to Karen's family. All of us sister-friends remained close and in contact often via Skype.

Karen now had three children—Sarah, nine years old (Jack's best friend), and two little boys, three and five years old. When we were in Santa Fe, Mike and I spent much time with Karen and Coyote. Of course, during the time there, all of us older folks spent hours among all the children, including Maria's family. We were their aunts and uncles, and we'd become one extensive happy family.

I was worried about Grandmother, though. She was Coyote's real-life grandmother and had been Isabella's and my mother in a past life and Karen's sister in a different past life. I felt blessed each time I saw Grandmother, who was now quite old and hadn't been feeling particularly well lately. I was anxious to get to Santa Fe to see how she was faring.

The exciting thing was that Isabella, Nica, and Angela were now business partners in Angela's new boutique opening in Santa Fe's center in a few days. It was thanks to Cal that the store even came into being. He'd been looking for a way to help the three girls realize their dreams. An excellent way to satisfy each was for Angela to have her store, providing Nica with a place to display her artwork. Isabella would use her business skills as she oversaw the financial end of things for Angela. Cal had been generous in providing them with an interest-free, open-ended loan.

Since graduating from college, Isabella had become adept with all the financial aspects of running a business and was determined to teach Angela what she needed to know. Isabella now partnered with me in running Cal's Trust and was free from a strict 9 a.m. to 5 p.m. schedule, allowing her to give Roberto a hand when needed.

We all were looking forward to heading to Santa Fe. The taxi had arrived to take us to the airport, but Jack was missing. We stood at the bottom of the stairs waiting for him.

"C'mon, Jack, hurry it up!" urged Mike.

"Coming, Daddy, I forgot my baseball glove."

Hearing that, Mike winked at me. Jack always forgot things—lost in the clouds as I'd been as the little Native American Indian girl, Little Bird.

Jack ran down the stairs with a wide grin. "Here I am."

"C'mon, son, let's go," Mike said, pushing him forward with his hand on Jack's shoulder. "We don't want to be late."

I watched the two of them walk to the waiting car outside. It was remarkable how much they looked alike, considering that Mike wasn't Jack's birth father. Thank God Mike was the man he was. It hadn't been easy for him to discover that fact ...

\*\*\*

When Mike and I strolled with Jack in the center of town the last time we were in Santa Fe, an Indian woman halted her walk toward us and stared at Jack. Noting our confusion, she said in embarrassment, "Please don't mind me, but your little boy looks exactly like someone I knew as a child."

"Oh?" responded Mike.

"He even has his swagger," she chuckled.

"Is that right?" asked Mike. "Is it someone we might know?"

"Probably not. Sorry to bother you," the woman said, patting Jack on the head before walking away.

"That was odd," said Mike, bewildered.

"Maybe she meant my heaven father," Jack said. Excited to see the taco wagon, he pulled on my hand and asked, "Can I get a taco, Mama?"

Mike lagged behind, lost in thought, and my heart fell. I knew we were headed for a long-overdue conversation about Jack's birth, and I had no idea what I'd say to him.

"Mike, do you want a taco, too?" I asked.

"Sure," he said in a quiet voice.

When we returned home, Jack went off to play, and Mike said, "Can we talk, Rosie?"

"Sure, sweetheart."

"What did Jack mean when he said, 'my heaven father'?"

I flushed. "Let's sit down, shall we?" Sitting at the kitchen table, I reached for Mike's hand. "Several years ago, I stood outside Jack's bedroom and heard him talking. When I went into his room, there was no one there. When I asked him who he was talking to, he answered that he was talking to his "heaven" father."

"Who is this "heaven" father?" asked Mike, curious.

"Since then, I've had several visions, and I think it's Tom Little Horse."

Silence took over as Mike began to put the puzzle pieces together. Finally, he asked, "Is Tom Little Horse Jack's father?"

"We won't know for sure unless we have a DNA test done on Jack. But it's a possibility. If you remember that summer ...."

"That damn summer ..." groaned Mike.

"When I discovered I was pregnant, I asked Grandmother if she knew who the father of my baby was, and she said to tell you that your son was on his way. And, Mike, there is no denying he has been your son since birth."

"Does Jack know I'm not his real father?" Mike asked.

"What a silly question! Of course, you're his real father! He loves and adores you ...."

"You know what I mean, Rosie," he interrupted.

I studied Mike. "Let's ask him, then."

We called Jack to come, and he ran into the kitchen and stood by Mike's side. "What is it, Daddy?"

"Can you tell me about your "heaven" father?" Mike asked.

"Okay. What do you want to know?"

"What's his name?"

"Tom Little Horse. He's my "heaven" father, and you're my "earth" father," he said, grabbing Mike around the neck and hugging him. "Why?"

"Daddy didn't know about your "heaven" father," I said.

"Oh," Jack said, tightening the grip around Mike's neck. "I love you, Daddy."

"And I love you, my son," Mike said, pulling Jack into his lap and hugging him tightly. Mike became too emotional to say more. He turned to me with teary eyes and smiled, willing to accept things as they were.

# CHAPTER 13

T he day after we arrived in Santa Fe, Isabella and I drove to the town center and parked behind The Chic Boutique, the girls' new store. I hoisted the smaller two boxes I'd shipped to Santa Fe from Las Vegas while Isabella grabbed the larger one—filled with stunning hand-knitted jacket shawls. They were colorful and eye-catching, like many of the showy items of Las Vegas couture.

I was excited to see the store inside, especially now that it was freshly painted and nearly stocked. The back door opened before we got to it, and Maria welcomed us with a proud smile. She was there to help Angela unload the boxes of new merchandise and steam-press the clothes. Angela would price the articles, and Isabella would record them into inventory on the computer. Nica was already inside, unloading some of her artwork for sale. Karen would soon help her hang her pieces and deliver the jewelry items Grandmother wanted to sell.

I kissed Maria's cheek as she removed the box from my grasp. I stepped inside and marveled at the place. The inside of the store reeked of style and uniqueness. It was where a woman of any age could find a treasure—if she were willing to step away from the mundane and boring. Santa Fe was filled with artists who valued creativity and the beauty of unique items, and the younger women wanted to wear more of what the larger cities were showing. I smiled. The girls would be very successful, I thought.

The colors inside were light and airy—light grey walls and the stunning Indian-designed sturdy carpet on the floor would complement Nica's artwork. A large antique cherry wood cupboard was centered on one wall and stood open with several drawers spilling out items for purchase. The shelves on top were stocked with lightweight sweaters and colorful logo shirts. Racks of dresses, pants, and tops edged the store in neat white wooden boxed-in areas, and several free-standing racks stood in the middle of the store filled with beautiful items. A white enclosed case beneath the two cash registers held shelves of stunning handmade jewelry with reasonable prices. But the piece de resistance was a separate area in the back where two glass doors drew your eye to look beyond it to beautiful gowns and other clothes hanging there. It was like a large closet with items inside that took your breath away when you opened the doors. There were four dressing rooms—two on either side of the closet. You needed permission to see the clothes, and it was only one of the salesladies who could show you the very exclusive items. These were the couture items for both dress and casual—items that Louie was supplying.

Angela eyed me as I took in everything about the store. "Well, Auntie Rose?"

I hugged her tight. "My God, girl, look what you have created!"

"So, you like it?"

"Like it? I *love* it! It's gorgeous, my darling girl," I proclaimed as I kissed her.

Karen rushed through the door, out of breath. "Sorry, I'm late. The boys wanted me to bring one of the new puppies for Jack, but I knew Sweet Pea would be unhappy with that. She's the queen, after all. It took me time to convince the boys to leave the puppy behind. God, Rosie, Mike is a saint for looking after the kids today! They are full of beans—Mexican jumping beans, to be exact."

We laughed. We were well aware of the energy of the two small boys. "How is Grandmother doing?" I asked Karen.

"Pretty good. She's looking forward to seeing you later. Where's Nica?"

"I'm right here, Aunt Karen, in the back," she hollered, stepping forward to be seen.

"I can't wait to see which paintings you've chosen to hang. Let's get started!"

Karen was a fan of all of Nica's creations. And what was there not to like? Her paintings were an odd mixture of old and contemporary in bright colors and quickly caught your eye with their beautiful uniqueness. Already, she was making a name for herself.

While they got busy, Maria and I began to help Angela and Isabella unpack the boxes in the back room. Soon, three short knocks came on the back door, and we heard a male voice ask, "Anyone there?"

Angela turned toward the door with a smile. "C'mon in and see for yourself!"

It was her new boyfriend, Harry. He came inside with an air of confidence. "Hi there, y'all."

Harry was several years older than Angela and was good-looking in a Brad Pitt sort of way. Although I knew that neither Isabella nor Nica was that crazy about him, Angela was enthralled with him. Something about him bothered me as well ... an undercurrent of anger that could be trouble.

"Wow, it looks like you got a lot more stuff in, Angie."

She nodded, pleased.

"What's this?" he asked, picking up a silver bracelet and trying it on. "How much is this?"

Isabella reached for it. "It's not for sale. Sorry."

"Hey, you don't need to grab it from me, Bella!" he warned.

"Stop calling me Bella. That's not my name," she scolded.

"Okay, okay, I won't," Harry promised, his hands held in a defensive mode. "Hey, Angie, are we still on for tonight?"

"Sure," she replied, her cheeks reddening.

"Okay, I'll call you later."

He kissed Angela on the cheek and turned to us. "Later."

Once the door closed behind him, the air became thick with tension. Angela turned to the other girls. "I know you two don't like Harry, but I do. Can you at least give us a break long enough to see where this is going?"

Isabella and Nica hung their heads. "Sorry," Isabella said.

"Me, too," said Nica. "I just don't trust him."

"You've made your point, and I get it. Come on, everyone, we have much more work to do," Angela urged.

Maria was quiet, and Karen and I remained silent. There was nothing more to say.

# CHAPTER 14

A fter lunch, I excused myself and went to see Grandmother. I walked the pathway to her condo when I arrived at the Pueblo. I wasn't surprised to find her standing in the doorway, waiting for me. Her psychic abilities were still keen.

"Good afternoon, Grandmother—my mother!"

"Good afternoon, my daughter. I'm glad to see you. Come on inside. I have tea waiting for us."

I watched as Grandmother eased herself with some difficulty into her chair at the table as I poured each of us a cup of tea. After I sat down, she pushed the waiting plate of homemade cookies toward me. I took one and bit into it. She smiled to see the pleasure on my face. Her cookies were the best because she always added her special spices.

"So, my child, how are you?" Grandmother asked.

I eyed her artfully. "Things are okay. I told you that Mike knows now that Tom Little Horse is Jack's birth father, didn't I?"

She nodded.

"Back then, why did you say to tell Mike that his son was on the way, Grandmother? Did you know that wasn't true?"

"My child, is Jack not Mike's son?"

"Yes, but ..."

She patted my hand. "Sometimes, we must be willing to look at the larger picture before we say what seems obvious. If I'd told you the baby was from Tom Little Horse's seed, it would have taken away Mike's joy of being a father and your joy of giving him a child. Things get righted in time. Now the two of them have grown even closer knowing the truth, have they not?"

I nodded and reached for another cookie, lost in thought. "How are you doing, Grandmother? How are you feeling?"

"My bones are tired, but my spirit is strong. I have my family from the past and my family today to enjoy. I'm very blessed."

"As we are to have you in our lives, Grandmother."

I spotted a twinkle in her eye. "You needn't worry, Rosie. I'll not join the Great Spirit for many days."

"That's good news, Grandmother," I replied with noticeable relief.

"There is much left to do. For one, the three girls have their store opening, and I promised Nica I'd go."

I smiled. "Yes, and the girls would be upset if you missed being there. By the way, Grandmother, what do you think of Angela's boyfriend?"

"Ahh. You need to warn Angela to be careful. She needs to see for herself that he is not right for her. She will have to stand up to him, and he won't like it."

"I was afraid you'd say something like that. Luckily, all three girls have taken extensive self-defense classes."

"They all must be careful," Grandmother added with a knowing look.

I shivered at her words.

Sliding her cup toward me, Grandmother asked, "Will you please pour me more tea, my daughter? These old bones like the warmth."

After refilling our cups, I asked, "Is Nica driving you to the opening tomorrow night?"

"No, I'm going with Karen and Coyote."

"That's nice. Jack will be spending the night with their kids here. I hope the babysitter knows what she's getting into," I chuckled.

Grandmother smiled. "Karen has her hands full." Sipping the last of her tea, Grandmother took my hand. "Help me up, please. I want to show you something."

"What is it, Grandmother?"

I followed her into her bedroom. She went to one of the two smaller drawers atop her chest. She pulled out a photo and showed it to me. It was a picture of a beautiful Indian girl, a younger version of Grandmother, and a fierce-looking man staring into the camera with a serious expression. "Is this you, Grandmother? And who is that man? Jack looks exactly like him."

"Yes, that's me and my husband—not a very happy man—and not a very happy marriage—while it lasted. I'm showing you this because the man was Tom Little Horse's grandfather, and I thought you might want to know that."

"You never talk about your husband."

"No, he had the same kind of anger that Angela's new boyfriend has."

"I'm sorry, Grandmother, things weren't better for you."

She held the picture out to me. "Someday, you might want to show Jack this picture."

I pushed her hand back. "Maybe. Not today, though."

"No, not today," she agreed intuitively.

# CHAPTER 15

**"** Mama, did Grandfather call you for directions to the Chic Boutique? You know how he is. He and Virginia are always getting lost around here."

"All set, Isabella. Mike will pick them up when he returns from dropping Jack off at the Pueblo. Do you want to go with us, or are you driving there yourself?"

"I'll drive myself. I'm heading out now."

"Okay, we'll see you there shortly. You look lovely, my sweet girl. It's too bad that Sammy couldn't make the opening, but it's good that he's finishing up at the police academy. Has he made up his mind yet whether he's going to work for Roberto before joining Mike?"

"Not yet. Sammy wants to talk to Mike first." She kissed me goodbye. "I'm off, Mama."

Watching her walk away, I became overwhelmed with gratitude for Isabella being in my life. In large part, I had

Maria to thank for that, and I would always be indebted to her for her kindness and love. I'd grown to love Maria like a dear sister—another sister-friend.

In their early 20s, all three girls had grown into beautiful young ladies, physically and in spirit. In some ways, as the oldest, Isabella was still looked upon as the leader of their threesome. As the wise woman with psychic abilities, Isabella was counted upon for guidance by the other two when needed. And that was fine with her.

Nica was the most confident of the three, not affected by any criticism of her artwork; she didn't care what others thought of it or her. She created and painted as an expression of herself, which was enough for her. I smiled at the thought that it would take a strong man to appreciate her self-reliance.

Angela was losing her shyness and coming into her own. Although she sometimes swallowed her feelings, she'd become stronger in speaking her mind. Angela was creative in a different way than Nica. She didn't sew herself but had a knack for putting together others' creations in ways that caught the eye. She had an instinct for what clothing and jewelry pieces would look good on others, and she loved that challenge. It would be interesting to see how her relationship with Harry would turn out.

I heard Mike pull into the driveway, and I hurried outside. Cal was sitting up front, and Virginia was in the back. I opened the back door and climbed in. "Hi there, Cal and Virginia. So glad you're here. I know how busy you are trying to move into your new condo. Do you like it better than the one you had before?"

Virginia's smile said it all. "It's wonderful. I can't wait for you to see it."

Cal said, "This new complex is practically next door to you. Easy for you now to walk over and see us. You'll have to check it out."

"That's great. Jack will love knowing you're nearby. And Isabella, too, of course," I said. "We're so used to being neighbors in Vegas that it feels strange when you're not right next door here."

"The girls must be excited about the opening," Virginia said.

"Wait until you see what the girls have done. You're going to love it!"

When we reached the boutique, parking was out of control. Mike dropped us off at the front door and searched for parking. It was exciting to see all the men with sports jackets and the women dressed up. I was looking forward to joining them.

Once inside, there were a few couples I didn't recognize, new to the area and owners of some of the high-end houses recently built on the hills outside the city. Santa Fe was becoming more and more popular as a place to live. I caught the eye of several couples, long-time residents in the valley, and waved to them.

The caterers wore black and white and skirted around the people to hand out glasses of champagne and offer hors d'oeuvres. I took a glass of champagne and handed it to Virginia while Cal reached for another one and handed it to me. I smiled at him, and he winked. He then took a glass for himself from the pretty girl who'd waited.

I saw Maria at the cash registers ringing up a purchase for a lady while Isabella showed jewelry to two other women. Nica was busy explaining a painting to one of the newer couples in town, and Karen held it up so they could step back and appraise it. Angela was in the center of the store, holding up an outfit for all to see. Then, she placed it back on the rack and pulled out another duo. Soon, I saw two women grab what Angela had shown and clutch the pieces in their arms. Already, the sales were pouring in. Angela was moving toward the back of the store, and I knew where she was heading.

"C'mon, you two," I said to Virginia and Cal. "I want you to see something."

We tagged behind a group of women intent on following Angela wherever she went. Angela stood beside the glass doors of the closeted area and spoke. "For those looking for something special and unique, welcome to the Magic Closet. It is our couture section with items from the designer Louie of Las Vegas. No one is allowed in this room without a sales clerk. If you want to see the items, ask one of them to assist you. Right now, though, I will show you several items to give you an idea of our styles."

I chuckled. Yes, quiet Angela had come a long way in climbing out of her shell. She knew what she was doing. Just by saying no one was allowed inside, Angela had whetted the appetite for the women to want to see it all.

Virginia stepped closer to Angela when she held up a casual dress that was her style and would look great on her. She raised her arm to get Angela's attention and asked, "What size is that? If it's a size 10, I want it."

That was all it took. Pretty soon, several women were pushing forward to look closely at it. "Are there any more like that?" a lady asked.

"Not exactly, but there's one in another print. What size are you looking for?" Angela asked. Spotting me, she said, "Rosie will help you try it on."

I felt Mike at my elbow. "You've got your work cut out for you with this one, sweetheart," he whispered because we both recognized her as one of the problematic locals.

I handed him my glass of champagne and said, "Wish me luck."

Hours later, when the store had cleared out, I plopped down on one of the chairs around the shop for customers to rest. I was bone tired. Grandmother was seated in the chair next to me. Mike had gone ahead with Virginia, Cal, Miguel, and Coyote to claim a table at our favorite restaurant that'd recently moved into a different space. We'd join them shortly.

"What do you think, Grandmother? It doesn't look like there's much left."

She chuckled. "The girls did alright, didn't they?"

"Quite a bit of your jewelry sold, too."

A proud smile crossed her face. "Yes."

Harry came through the doorway and looked around. Angela saw him and came forward to greet him.

"Wow, you cleared out a lot of stuff. How much money did you make, Angie?" he asked.

Angela's cheeks reddened. "Hush," she said, pulling him further into the store after she gave him a quick kiss.

He looked around. "Look at this place. There's nothing left!" he said as he grabbed a glass of champagne off a tray left on the counter near the cash registers.

Isabella was behind the counter, straightening up the jewelry. She had placed some of it on the shelf above while she wiped down the inside of the cabinet. Harry picked up a bracelet and put it on his wrist.

"Can I have this?" he asked Angela.

"Give it back, Harry. It doesn't belong to you," demanded Isabella.

"It doesn't belong to you, either. All this stuff belongs to Angie."

Angela looked mortified. Isabella rolled her eyes but didn't dispute what he'd said. Instead, she held her hand out. "Give me the bracelet, Harry. It belongs to Grandmother."

"Grandmother? You mean that wrinkled old lady in the corner?" he whispered loudly.

"Just give it to me, please," Isabella demanded.

"I didn't like it anyhow," he said, tossing it back to her.

Nica came to stand by Angela. "You're wanted in the back. A customer needs your help."

"I've got to go anyway, Angie. I'm meeting up with the guys," he said, gulping down the last of the champagne and making a face. "Whew! Too warm to taste good."

Angela watched him leave. With her hands on her hips, she looked between the two girls. "No customer needs my help, right?"

"Right," Nica and Isabella said as one.

"Someday, Angela, I swear if you don't kill him, I will," declared Nica. "He's such a shit."

Hearing her words, I felt goosebumps cover my body. Grandmother had listened to what she'd said as well. When I turned to her, she sat with her eyes closed, silently mouthing Tewa words. After finishing, she looked at me with worried eyes.

Angela stood there, embarrassed. "I don't know why you two don't want anyone to know you're my business partners."

"That's the whole idea of being silent partners," smiled Isabella. "C'mon, let's get our mothers and Grandmother and join the others for our celebration. Since tomorrow is Sunday and we open later, we can come back in the morning to clean up."

The restaurant had reserved a small room off the main dining area for our celebration party. Although now in a different location, the restaurant was the same one where Romano had been invited to be a guest chef all those years ago. Fortunately for us, the same chef was still with the restaurant, and no matter what we chose to eat, I knew it'd be delicious. My stomach growled in anticipation as we headed out the door to join the others.

# CHAPTER 16

**M**ike and I found ourselves alone the following day, which was unusual. Jack had spent the night with Karen and Coyote's kids, and Isabella had spent the night at Nica's. We made slow, easy love that was delicious without any interruptions. Our desire for each other hadn't waned, and it was always with great joy to realize how lucky I was to have Mike in my life.

"Ready for a cup of coffee?" he asked.

"Yup, it's beautiful weather. We can sit out on the deck with it."

"Okay then, Sleepy Head, time to get up," he teased, pulling me out of bed. He love-patted my backside, pushing me forward.

Sipping our coffee outside, I said, "Karen invited us for lunch. What do you think?"

Mike was lost in thought.

"Mike?"

"Oh, sorry. I was thinking about Cal. He looked worn out last night. The move must be tiring him out."

"I agree. Maybe instead of going to Karen and Coyote's, we should see what we can do to give Cal a hand with their move. He looked peaked."

"Great idea. They're close enough now that we can walk there."

"Sounds good to me," I said. "Besides, I need the exercise."

As we neared the new property, the old Santa Fe-styled three-story building was stunning in its simplicity. Even the yard was attractive with the desert plantings. Their first-floor condo had easy access near the back. After knocking at the door, Virginia opened it with a wide smile. "C'mon in. I'll start the coffee."

The condo was beautiful, and I loved it! We stepped into a terracotta-tiled entrance, expanding to the hallway that opened up to all the rooms in the house with the same flooring throughout. There were two bedrooms with full baths, a small open area for an office, a large living room with a stone fireplace centered between built-in bookshelves, a stunning kitchen/dining area with an island big enough for two people to eat there, white wooden cabinets, black marble countertops, and stainless-steel appliances. The piece de resistance was the enclosed patio that brought the outside in, adding a cozy, comfortable extra room to the well-laid-out floor plan.

Virginia, known for brewing her famous Mexican coffee, was moving around in the kitchen. As we stood in the living room, the aroma of the coffee reached us, and we looked at each other and automatically moved toward the kitchen. We sat at the table, sipping the coffee and talking for a few minutes before Mike got up and announced, "Okay, Cal, let's see what we can do about emptying some more boxes. Lead the way."

Virginia and I tackled the kitchen while they unloaded books and installed them on the bookshelves. We opened several boxes and put dishes, glasses, and cookware away in the many available cabinets. When we were nearly finished, Mike called anxiously from the living room.

"Rosie, come quick! I think Cal has fainted!"

I ran into the living room with Virginia at my heels. Cal was flat on his back, not moving, and my heart raced with fear. Looking closer, I could see his chest rise and fall as he breathed, and relief washed over me. Virginia grabbed my shoulder and leaned into me. She had her other hand pressed against her mouth in worry. Cal began to move, and after a few seconds, he sat up.

"What happened?" he asked.

"I think you fainted," Mike said.

"Let's get you checked out," I said. "C'mon."

"That's not necessary," he protested.

"You are going to the hospital whether you like it or not, and we don't want to hear another word about it," scolded Virginia. "Mike, can you please help him to the car."

"We're going with you," I demanded.

"I'll drive," Mike added.

Most times at the hospital, getting held up with paperwork is easy before they allow you to see a doctor. However, when we arrived with Cal, he was rushed inside for an EKG while we did the necessary paperwork. We sat for nearly two hours in the waiting before a doctor approached us with Cal behind him, looking slightly tousled.

"Cal's a lucky man. He had a slight heart attack, a myocardial infarction, and it's a warning. He needs to improve his diet and exercise routine, or he will be in trouble." He turned back to Cal. "Make sure to see your doctor when you get home. We've already forwarded the test results to him."

Shaken, Cal nodded in agreement.

"Thank you, doctor. I'll make sure we both eat better and exercise more," promised Virginia.

"That's good. Cal, you're young yet and have a lot to live for, so follow my advice if you want to make it into your 90s and beyond."

The doctor's advice was sobering news for all of us. No more, "I'll start to get in shape tomorrow." It had to begin today for all of us.

# CHAPTER 17

T hat summer was a time of change for many of us. After spending two weeks with us, Mike left to return to Las Vegas. Sammy had decided not to wait and signed on to go into detective work with Mike and Brian right after graduating from the police academy. He would make the third detective in the Las Vegas office, as Mike had hired an older man two years ago. Roger Mayberry was perfect for any stakeout work because he didn't mind being alone or working odd hours. I found Roger somewhat of a shy, gentle soul, more interested in helping people get their life in order than anything else.

Isabella had flown back with Mike. She and Sammy had moved into the guest house where Virginia had lived before joining Cal in the main house. Now that Sammy had secured his dream job with Mike, I wondered if he and Isabella would move forward and get married, as they had discussed previously. They had talked about a spring wedding. My heart fluttered at the thought. Their marriage wouldn't surprise anybody since she and Sammy committed to each other years ago. But to have them finally married seemed impossible. Where had the years gone?

I awoke to an empty house of people, and it felt odd. Sweet Pea nudged me and flopped over onto her back on the bed. She hoped I'd rub her tummy and made happy sounds of pleasure as I patted her. I laughed, watching her. She knew how to work it because I did exactly as she commanded. I sure did love her.

After a bit, I left the bed, let Sweet Pea outside, and made coffee. It would be a beautiful summer day, and I was looking forward to visiting Karen and Coyote's new place at the Pueblo. They had built a large two-story home where all the kids loved to hang out. Jack was already there, having spent the night with Sarah and her brothers. Jack loved to be with the other kids instead of home alone with just me, and who could blame him?

My phone rang, and I smiled when I saw it was Mike. "Hi, Sweetheart!"

"Hi, yourself. Everything okay there?"

"Yup. I was thinking about Isabella and Sammy. I think they will get married in the spring, as they said. Have they mentioned anything to you about it?"

Mike paused. "Maybe you should talk to Isabella."

"Why? What's up?" I asked, concerned.

"I don't want to say anything. Just talk to Isabella. Call me later, okay?"

My heart pounded. What was wrong? I envisioned Isabella in tears. I tapped in Isabella's cell phone number and waited and waited while the phone rang and rang. I hung up, and after a few minutes, I tried again. Once more, the phone rang and rang, and I was just about to give up when I heard a snuffle at the last minute. "Hello?"

"Isabella, is that you? What's wrong?"

"Oh, Mama, it's all my fault. Sammy wants to get married right away, and I want to wait. I want a big wedding, as I've always dreamed about, and Sammy wants a small family wedding as soon as possible. We've argued, and now we're not speaking to each other." Between sobs, she whined, "He didn't even sleep here last night. He said I needed time to rethink what was important—us being together."

"Oh, Isabella, I'm so sorry. So, what are you going to do?"

She gave a small laugh. "I'm going to lie down. I'm exhausted."

"That sounds like a good idea," I said.

"Can I call you later, Mama?"

"Of course, darling. Maybe we can look at the situation in a different light then, too."

"Goodbye, Mama. I love you."

"I love you, too, my beautiful Little One."

My heart dropped at the thought of what Isabella was going through, but I knew she and Sammy would work it out. They had good conflict resolution skills, which had been proven on occasion. I just needed to stay out of it, which would be hard for me to do.

I rang Mike back, and it went straight into voice mail. I'd have to catch up with him later. I went inside and popped into the shower, letting the water run over me until it eased some of my stress. Then, I got dressed and scooped up Sweet Pea, sitting at my feet, sensitive to my mood. We loaded into the car and headed to Karen's house.

\*\*\*

Sitting on her back deck with a fresh mug of Mexican coffee, we could hear Sarah, Jack, and a neighbor child playing a card game on the far side while the younger boys raced around in the backyard.

"What's wrong, Rosie?" asked Karen, studying me.

"I didn't realize it showed," I said worriedly. "I talked to Isabella this morning, and she and Sammy argued last night about their getting married."

"That doesn't sound like them," Karen said.

"Isabella has always wanted a big wedding while Sammy wants a small one with just family."

Karen chuckled. "Isabella's family isn't that small. Maybe that's what is on his mind."

I smiled. "There's that too. But Sammy wants to get married immediately instead of a spring wedding as they'd discussed earlier."

"I wonder why now?" asked Karen. "Hasn't he just started his job with Mike?"

A thought came to me. "Karen, you're right; that makes sense. The more I think about it, it makes perfect sense."

"What does?" she asked, confused. "What did I say?"

"Since Sammy's new job can be dangerous, I think he wants to make sure that nothing happens to stop him from marrying Isabella, and that's why he wants to get married right away."

"I see where you are coming from," Karen said, nodding in agreement.

I sat back in my chair and felt much of the tension in my shoulders leave. A shuffle at the end of the deck caught our attention. Sarah was standing over the board game. She wrapped her arm around Jack's neck and bent to kiss his cheek. "You're going to marry me one day, Jack," she stated. "Just wait and see."

"Sure," agreed Jack. "Now, let's finish the game, okay? I'm winning."

Karen and I looked at each other, shaking our heads. The two of them had a connection. What Sarah said wouldn't surprise us if that came to be. Jack was crazy about Sarah, but I doubted Sarah would settle until she outgrew some of her wanderlust.

"You'll see," Sarah persisted.

Karen and I just looked at each other and smiled. It seemed that I wasn't the only one thinking about a wedding.

# CHAPTER 18

I t turned out that my assumption of why Sammy wanted to get married so soon was correct. He'd said that he'd waited long enough to become man and wife, and there was no sense waiting any longer, especially in light of his new job. Once Isabella and Sammy had talked things over, she agreed to his wish. She loved him, and as long as her closest friends would be at the wedding, what did the timing matter? For Sammy to feel the urgency to get married worried me because, with his psychic abilities, did he know something I didn't?

They set a date for the end of August, and with most of the people we considered as family living in Santa Fe, it made no sense to have the wedding any other place.

Since the wedding was now only weeks away, Isabella would fly back to Santa Fe to make the necessary arrangements. She had already talked to Louie about making her dress and the dresses for Nica and Angela as bridesmaids, and he'd agreed. Isabella's dress would be beautiful in a cocktail-length elegant style made of charmeuse satin. The girls' dresses were simple in design, each in a different style but made of the same silk in a shade of eggplant. Because the dresses were going to be designed by Louie, he'd arranged for a noted photographer to photograph his creations for a spread in one of the high-end magazines. At first, we'd objected to the notoriety but finally had agreed to Louie's request in return for his kindness in designing the dresses for the wedding party.

Sammy's parents would arrive a week before the wedding. They would stay with Cal and Virginia in their new condo. Since Sammy's parents had no siblings and Sammy was an only child, they had spent many happy times and holidays with us during the past few years. They were like family to us all. I smiled, thinking of the two of them. I couldn't have found a better person to be the other "mother-in-law" than Maggie Brooks. I adored her, and we loved sharing our kids. Maggie's husband, David, was a great guy and had become one of Mike's closest friends.

There was a new Bed and Breakfast Inn in town, and I immediately called to book it entirely for our out-of-town wedding guests. My other sister-friends had already booked into the Eldorado Resort Hotel and Spa, where they'd often stayed when visiting. Romano and Randy, Mimi and Charles, Louie and his partner, and the photographer would be staying at the inn. Sammy and some of his friends would stay there too. Brian would be staying with us.

I drove to Albuquerque to pick up Isabella at the airport with Jack and Sweet Pea in the back seat. Interestingly, although Sweet Pea showed her love for Jack, it was Isabella to whom the dog was attached. Jack was aware of it and complained now and then about wanting his own dog. Maybe it was time to get him one, I thought.

Karen had mentioned holding one of her dog's puppies aside for him. She was a cross between a black miniature poodle and a silky, like Sweet Pea. The pups' father had been a wandering visitor and had left a surprise behind when Karen's dog had delivered the pups. The puppies were adorable, with silky, curly black hair. I'd have to talk to Mike about the dog, and if he agreed, we'd pick up the puppy after the wedding. She'd be old enough then.

We pulled into the passenger pick-up area at the airport to find Isabella waiting for us.

"Hi, Mama! Hey, buddy, how's it going? Hi Sweet Pea, my sweet little girl."

"Hi, Bella," said Jack, saying the nickname only he was allowed to use. "Where's Sammy?"

"Oh, he won't be here for a few weeks. He's working with Mike."

"I wish I could work with Daddy, too," Jack said in disappointment.

"Well, maybe someday you will."

"Maybe …."

"Mama, you won't believe how beautiful the dresses Louie designed are! He's a genius! He said to tell you he's also sending you a dress, and he's making one for Maggie, too."

"Really? He's going all out, huh? That's wonderful!"

"Louie is excited about being featured in the Living in Style magazine. By the way, the photographer is coming here in a day or two to get the lay of the land. He wants to see where we're going to have the wedding. When I spoke with him over the phone, he seemed nice but a bit uptight.

I told him we'd have him for dinner one night. I hope you don't mind."

"Not at all. Happy to do it."

***

A few days later, Isabella received a telephone call from Jeff Greenfield, the Living in Style magazine photographer, wanting to meet with her. Isabella asked Nica to join them, and I smiled at the thought. Skeptical of anyone not doing it justice, Nica would have her own idea of how to show off the Pueblo in the best light. Jeff Greenfield would have his hands full with those two girls.

Later in the afternoon, Isabella drove to the house, and Jack and Sweet Pea raced out the door. An extremely handsome young man appeared from the back of the car and stretched his long legs. I thought he was a bit older than the girls—possibly in his late 20s or early 30s. He had rusty-colored hair and wore black-rimmed glasses around bright blue eyes that made him appear studious. However, when he laughed at Sweet Pea's playfulness, the child in him emerged, making me smile. Isabella and Nica exited the car and watched Jeff fuss over Sweet Pea and Jack.

I stepped forward and held out my hand. "Hi, Jeff, I'm Rosie. It looks like you all have had a full afternoon. Come in, and I'll give you a nice cold drink before dinner."

As a group, we all moved forward. Noting Nica's flushed cheeks, I asked, "How are you, sweetheart?"

Nica nodded toward the photographer's back as he walked ahead with Jack beside him. She rolled her eyes. "It's been a long afternoon," she answered.

I chuckled. Isabella came to my side and whispered, "Just watch them."

Inside, I fixed margaritas and went outside to join the three of them as they stretched out on the lounge chairs on the deck. Jack had gone to watch his program on television, and Sweet Pea cuddled next to Isabella. Charged energy passed between Nica and Jeff, and I wasn't sure why.

"So, how did it go?" I asked Jeff.

"Pretty well, considering."

Nica interjected. "He means, considering he had to deal with me."

Jeff flushed. "That too." His eyes twinkled. "Nica's not without an opinion, that's for sure."

It was Nica's turn to blush. "Well, I hate to see writers not get the history of the Pueblo correct."

"This is a gorgeous country in its own right," he continued. "I didn't realize New Mexico had so many Navajo pueblos. It's quite fascinating. Their Indian artwork is beautiful though somewhat primitive."

"Earthy is what I think you mean," Nica said, glaring at him.

Jeff tipped his head Nica's way and stared at her. After a few seconds filled with tension, he acknowledged her statement. "Exactly."

Isabella laughed. "You two. Calling Nica an earthy woman certainly did not win you any prizes, Jeff."

He laughed good-naturedly. "Obviously."

"Obviously," Nica added, smiling.

"What are your plans, Jeff? What will you do to get ready for the article?" I asked.

Seeking Nica's attention, he said, "I'm going to stick around for a bit to get more of a feel for this place. It's my first time here. I hope to get the ladies to show me around some more."

"Sorry, I have meetings tomorrow," Isabella said. "But maybe you can go with him, Nica?"

She flushed. "I guess so."

It was interesting to see Nica so flustered. Isabella winked at me. I knew she had no scheduled meetings and wondered what she was up to.

# CHAPTER 19

T he following day, I grabbed my mug of coffee and went outside on the deck. Isabella was already there. "Good morning, sweetheart. You're up early."

"Couldn't sleep. I'm going down to the Chic Boutique to work on the books. We've been so lucky to have such a good start. Angela said that she and the other sales girls can hardly keep up with everything because the store is so busy."

"That's for sure," I agreed. "So, what's up between Nica and Jeff?"

Isabella laughed. "Aren't they funny together? I've never seen Nica like this. And Jeff is gaga over her and loves to tease her. They laugh all the time, sometimes, at things I don't think are funny at all."

"Is that why you told Jeff you had meetings when you don't?"

She laughed again. "Did you see the relief on Jeff's face when I said that?"

I chuckled. "I thought so."

"Even though Nica is attracted to him, I can't imagine she'll let things get serious. You know how she wants to stay at the reservation and help her people out."

"All the Native American Indian tribes need strong advocates not to be run over by others wanting to take advantage of them … their land in particular."

"So true. What are you going to do today, Mama? Are you going down to the store to help out?"

"I thought I would. Maria asked if Jack wanted to come over and cook with Rosa. You know how well those two get along since they both love to eat!"

"Yes, they're cute together. Well, I will get dressed then and head down to the store. Since it's Saturday, we'll be busy," Isabella said as she rose from her chair and went inside.

\*\*\*

Later, I pulled into Maria's driveway. Both Jack and I got out and headed up to the house. Maria came to the door, looking beautiful with her new hairstyle that fell naturally in a shoulder-length cut. The years had brought out more of her inner beauty, and she was lovely, quickly catching the eye of more than her husband. Homelife with Miguel had changed too. It was easier now since he lived softer, a noticeable improvement from his angry past. Miguel now owned his successful landscaping business, which I thought helped.

"Hi, my sweet friend," I said as I kissed Maria's cheek. "Are you sure you're okay with having Jack here?"

"Rosa has been dying to learn to make more of the fancier Mexican dishes, and, of course, I wouldn't think of showing her without Jack being here."

"They are a pair, aren't they?"

Maria laughed. "Yes, they are. Are you heading down to the boutique?"

"I thought I would since it's Saturday. Angela is bound to have her hands full."

Maria frowned. "Her hands are full alright, with that Harry. I don't care for him, Rosie, and I've told Angela that, but if I say too much more, she'll rebel. I know she will."

"I agree. Just give her some time, and Angela will find out he isn't the one for her. Grandmother says that, too."

Maria rolled her eyes and grunted in displeasure.

"I'll be back later. Call me if you need me to pick up anything while I'm out," I said.

I pulled into the alleyway behind the store and parked my car. I slipped in the back door and could hear the shoppers out front making pleasing sounds. I smiled, thinking Angela was pulling together some outfits for them to view. I turned the corner and found Isabella sitting at the computer with a puzzled look.

"What's the matter, sweetheart?" I asked.

"I can't seem to balance everything out. I'm off a few dollars, but someone may have pushed the wrong button when a sale was made. I'll go over it again."

"How much are you off?" I asked.

"An even $50."

"Hmm. It's unusual to have it be an even number like that. I hope you can find it."

"Me, too."

I walked out front.

"Auntie Rose! You're here just in time. Will you show this customer the Magic Closet, please?"

"Of course, Angela. It'll be my pleasure."

By the end of the afternoon, I was tired and looking forward to getting off my feet. At closing time, Angela, Isabella, and I were left in the store when the door opened, and Harry walked in with his swagger.

"Angie, here?" he asked.

"Yes, she's in the back. Oh, here she is now!" I said as Angela and Isabella entered the front room.

Seeing Harry, Angela stepped forward to greet him. "Here to help me out again?" she asked sweetly.

"Why not?" he said as he kissed her cheek. He pushed some of Angela's hair behind her ear, and when he did, the shiny silver bracelet he wore came into view.

Recognizing it as the one he'd tried on before, Isabella asked, "Did you buy that bracelet, Harry?"

"It was a gift from Angie for helping her out last night," he said, staring into Angela's eyes, daring her to refute what he'd said.

Surprise crossed Angela's brow, and she blushed furiously.

"Is that right, Angela?" demanded Isabella.

Angela glared at Harry and nodded reluctantly. It was clear to everyone that he'd taken it without her permission.

"Why are you so bent out of shape, Isabella? All this belongs to Angie, and she can do with it what she wants," stated Harry.

"I'm afraid that's not true, Harry," announced Angie in a sad voice. "I have investors to answer to, so that you know."

"Whatever ..." he replied. "C'mon, let's go. The help can clean up."

"I'm afraid it doesn't work that way, Harry," Angela said.

"Well, I'm not hanging around where I'm not wanted. I'll catch you later, Angie," Harry said and left.

As soon as he went out the door, Angela burst into tears. "I'm so sorry. I didn't know."

Isabella was furious. "What about that missing money, Angela? I'm pretty sure that he took it," stated Isabella angrily.

"Is that true?" she asked, looking at Isabella and then at me. She was asking us to confirm it intuitively.

I nodded my head. "The trouble is, Angela, that unless you're willing to break off your relationship with him, he will continue to cause you problems. You must be very careful and ensure you're not left alone with him. He can't be trusted."

Fear crossed her face. "I'll lock up and make sure the alarm is set."

"Good idea. We'll wait here with you until that's done," I said.

"Maybe if I talk to him ..." Angela mumbled as she walked away.

Isabella and I looked at each other in frustration. Trouble was brewing.

# CHAPTER 20

J eff Greenfield was finally heading back to New York City the following day. He had spent a week in Santa Fe, and it was no secret that he had stayed because of Nica. It was easy for anyone to see Jeff falling in love with the strong-willed Indian girl who'd bewitched him with her native beauty. He appreciated her artistic talent and, at times, had sneaked up on her while she was working, photographing her as she created. He had taken many pictures of her artwork, intending to write a story about her for the magazine. Despite his attention, Nica had remained somewhat aloof, not wanting to get caught up in a romance that, in her mind, had no chance to move forward. She was not into a long-distance relationship, and so far, she had refused to entertain the idea of even a visit to New York City.

That night, I invited Jeff for dinner along with Nica and Angela. It was my way of thanking him for all the time he'd spent here to get the right background pictures for the wedding article. I knew he would do his best to make Louie shine, and I appreciated it. After dinner, they would meet some other friends at one of the local bars later for a final send-off for him.

Jeff arrived for dinner right on time. While Isabella and I were doing some last-minute chores, Jack entertained him by showing him some of his drawings. True to his good nature, Jeff explained what he liked about each one, causing Jack to smile with pleasure.

"Which one do you like best, Jeff?" Jack asked.

Immediately, Jeff picked out my favorite one as well—a scene of an older Indian man sitting in a rocking chair drawn from a photo taken at the Pueblo. Jack had talent and was signed up to take painting classes during the school year.

"Here, it's yours, then," stated Jack.

Jeff hesitated briefly before shaking Jack's hand and bowing low. "Thank you so much, Picasso."

Jack laughed at his joke.

When we heard the noise at the front door, Jack raced to it and walked back with Nica and Angela in tow. Behind them was Harry, whom I had not invited. Angela gave me a weak smile. "I hope you don't mind one more, Auntie Rose."

"Of course not," I said, trying to cover my annoyance.

Both Isabella and Nica looked unhappy.

"Hi there, Four Eyes. How's it going?" Harry asked Jeff.

Jack heard him. "That's not a nice thing to say."

"Is that right? Well, I can say whatever I want," Harry answered with annoyance.

"Not in this house, you can't! Just ask my mother."

We all burst out laughing, breaking up the tension in the room.

"Out on the deck, everyone. Margaritas will be coming your way," I ordered.

"No salt on mine," commanded Harry.

I ignored him and began gathering the things needed for the drinks.

"Did you hear me?" he demanded.

I looked at Harry in disbelief. "I certainly hope you're not talking to me in that tone. Please go outside, and I'll serve you in a few minutes."

"Touchy, are we?" he asked but walked outside as requested.

Angela stayed behind. "I tried not to bring him, but he insisted, Auntie Rose."

"You need to nip this in the bud, Angela. It's only going to get worst. Have you talked to your parents about this?"

"My mom."

"You need to discuss this with your father as well. Please do it as soon as possible, hear me?"

"Yes, Auntie Rose, I will, but …."

"But what?" I snapped.

"Nothing," she mumbled.

The evening was fun despite having Harry there. Studying him, I began to feel sorry for him because there was very little he could do or say that would change my mind about him. He was trouble—plain and simple. Harry came from a family with plenty of money, although I guessed not much of a secure unconditional sense of love. In some ways, he reminded me of Isabella and Sammy's classmate, Tiffany, who had a similar background and the same sense of entitlement. Each was a bully, although Tiffany was still in therapy to change her behavior.

After dinner, I said goodbye to Jeff and the others before they headed out. Isabella stayed back. "I'll help you clean up."

"No, go with the others and have fun. Jack and I will clean up."

"I'm only going to join them to be nice. I'd rather be home here with you. I don't want to be part of the trouble brewing, Mama. Do you feel it, too?"

"Yes, I do. Angela needs to be careful."

Isabella reluctantly left, and I stood in the kitchen by myself, wishing that Mike was here with me. Isabella was missing Sammy as well. Things seemed out of balance without the guys. Isabella was flying back to Las Vegas tomorrow night for a fitting of her dress. At the end of the week, she'd be returning to Santa Fe, and thankfully, Mike would be flying back with her. I couldn't wait to see him. Maybe he could talk some sense into Angela because she valued his opinion. We'd have to wait and see, I thought.

# CHAPTER 21

F or the next few days, I met with Karen, who was holding a shower for Isabella, who didn't want one. But it was part of the magazine spread featuring Louie's couture, and he'd created a new casual outfit for Isabella to wear that day. The rest of us would wear out-fits we'd chosen ourselves.

Karen had naturally put on a few pounds by having her three babies but in an overall pleasing way. Despite the extra weight, she was finally comfortable with her looks since Coyote loved her and her body just as it was. Being well-loved, Karen had grown more beautiful with age. Her tanned skin, dark hair, and eyes made her look more like a Native American Indian than most at the Pueblo. She'd chosen one of Louie's outfits from the store, as had I. So, despite not planning on it, we'd also be wearing Louie's designs at the shower and the wedding.

Preparing for the shower, Karen and I included Grandmother in some of the decisions, which pleased her. Plus, it gave her something to do since she spent less time selling her wares at the Governor's Palace. Eyeing her sitting with us, I realized what a treasure Karen had become to Grandmother. They got along so well, and each provided the other with a closeness of spirit that made me smile. They were not exactly "peas in a pod" but had a well-developed togetherness. I knew that their relationship pleased Coyote because he'd remarked on it.

"Are things pretty well set for the wedding, Rosie?" Karen asked.

"Yes, it will be very simple, just how they want it."

"You mean the way Sammy wants it, don't you?"

"Yes, but now Isabella is glad it will be just family. You know how she hates spending money if it's unnecessary," I chuckled.

Karen and Grandmother smiled and nodded.

"Becoming an accountant has done that to Isabella. She's conscientious about every penny spent through the Trust, and I have to tell you that I'm happy to have her take over that aspect of running it," I added.

"Yes, you're lucky to have her," agreed Karen. "You can trust her and not have to worry about having to keep an eye on someone else."

"You mean someone like Harry, don't you? I still can't get over him taking the bracelet without permission and saying it was Angela's thank-you gift, which surprised her. Trouble is brewing there, for sure."

Grandmother nodded but remained silent.

"Maria is worried as well. Is there anything we can do, Grandmother?" I asked.

"We have to allow the space for their journey whether we want to or not. Something is going to happen soon, so be prepared to step in then," Grandmother warned, holding her hand up to stop me from questioning her anymore.

Karen's two youngest, Thomas and Terence, came bounding into the kitchen where we were seated and stopped dead when they saw us looking so grim. "Mama, what's the matter?" asked Thomas, the older one by two years.

"Nothing, sweetheart," answered Karen. "Ready for some lunch? Do you want me to make you a picnic?"

"Yesss!" the boys screamed.

"You can eat it outside in your tent as long as you don't wander," she added.

They jumped up and down in agreement. "You have to mind me, Terence, since I'm older and the boss."

"He's not my boss, is he, Mama?" Terence asked, eyes watering in frustration.

"Listen, guys, why don't you each be the boss of yourself?"

The boys looked at each other and smiled. "Okay," they said, not grasping how Karen had out-maneuvered them.

I bit back a chuckle and turned away so the boys didn't see my smile. I saw Grandmother holding back a grin as well.

After they left, and we were nibbling on the sandwiches Karen had made for us, I asked the others, "Any update on Nica and Jeff?"

"Grandmother, you probably know more than I do," Karen said.

Grandmother shook her head. "She's a stubborn one."

"Isabella said that Jeff told Nica he was going to come to the wedding a few days early so that he'd have time to spend with her."

"Good luck with that ..." Karen added.

"Has Coyote been able to catch the thieves raising havoc in Santa Fe? Lots of petty crimes going on right now, I understand."

"All the shoplifting in town is adding up to being quite a lot of money, Coyote says. But the break-ins have him puzzled because they are bypassing the alarm systems. Initially, they were stealing things that were easy to turn over, but it seems like they've escalated into drugs or higher-end jewelry."

"That's not good," I said. "Coyote is smart enough to catch them when they least expect it," I assured them. "I don't doubt that."

Thinking of Harry and the robberies, a thought crossed my mind. I needed to remind Angela to change the code for the alarm system at the boutique.

# CHAPTER 22

A s we waited at Passenger Pickup at the Albuquerque airport for Mike and Isabella to come into view, I turned to Jack, sitting in the back of the car with Sweet Pea.

"Give Daddy a chance to get inside the car before you ask him about the puppy, okay?"

Jack bobbed his head in excitement. Sarah had let the cat out of the bag. When Karen had told a neighbor that the puppy she wanted wasn't available, Sarah had been curious to know why not. When asked, Karen had blurted out that the dog was reserved for Jack without thinking about what'd she said, and Sarah had told Jack. Of course, he was thrilled to hear the good news. I had bowed out of the decision-making, leaving it up to Mike to approve of Jack having the dog. Knowing Mike wouldn't object, I wanted him to be the hero.

Isabella laughed at something Mike said, and my heart swelled at seeing them approach. I exited the car and opened the trunk so they could pop in their suitcases. Isabella climbed into the back as Mike got into the front.

"Okay, Mama? Can I?" asked Jack.

I nodded while Mike looked at me curiously. "Jack has a very important question to ask you," I said.

"Hey, buddy, what's up?"

"Auntie Karen wants to give me one of the puppies when she's old enough. Can I keep her, Daddy?"

"A puppy is a pretty big responsibility. It's more than just feeding her. She'll depend upon you, and you'll need to spend a lot of time training her. Is that something you want to do?"

Jack was quiet for a minute. Then solemnly, he said, "Yes, I do, Daddy."

Mike looked at me and winked. "Okay, then. I guess you have yourself a new dog. You'll have to make sure that she gets along with Sweet Pea enough so we don't have a serious issue."

Isabella looked down at Sweet Pea in her lap and said, "You're up to having a little one around, aren't you, girl?" Sweet Pea stretched up and gave Isabella kisses. "That's a good girl," gushed Isabella.

"What are you going to name her, Jack?" Mike asked.

"Mama and I looked up Indian names. I think I'm going to call her Miko. Mama says it stands for a female shaman."

"That's a beautiful name, Jack. I love it," Isabella said.

"What do you think, Daddy?"

"I like it too, Jack."

I took my hand off the car wheel and reached for Mike's hand. He grasped it and squeezed it, turning to me with a smile. "I've missed you, my queen," he whispered.

"Not as much as I have missed you, handsome," I whispered.

At overhearing us, I saw Jack in the rear-view mirror put his finger in his open mouth as if he were gagging. Mike smiled and squeezed my hand tighter. I laughed out loud.

Back home, it was time to get serious about what must be done before the wedding. Sammy and his parents were flying in tomorrow. Cal and Virginia would pick them up at the airport and drive them back to their condo to stay. Sammy would be staying at the new B&B in town.

Cal and Virginia were walking each day and had cut down on sweets and fats. Cal had already lost five pounds, while Virginia had struggled to lose two. They had put their foot down when it came to not having a glass of wine at night. They enjoyed it too much to give it up, and a little red wine was good for them, anyway, the doctor agreed. Maggie and David would be happy because they'd become knowledgeable about wines and loved nothing more than a good wine at night.

Isabella was unpacking and called to me, "Mama, come see."

I left Mike and hurried into her bedroom, excited to see the dresses Louie had designed for us. As Isabella held up one dress after another, I was overcome to see their magnificence. Her wedding gown was exquisite in its simplicity and showed Isabella's beauty in all the best ways. The bridesmaid's gowns in their excellent shade of eggplant were perfect to counterbalance her dress. The dress Louie had designed for me was breathtaking in a design that would wrap around my waist, showing off its slimness and pronouncing my chest area. Very sexy but reserved at the same time. The richness of the honey-taupe color was an excellent enhancement to my skin color. I couldn't have been more pleased. Tears filled my eyes.

"Oh, Mama, are you okay?" Isabella asked.

"Louie did such a beautiful job for us. Your wedding is going to be so beautiful, Isabella! I'm so happy for you."

"Yes, Louie is beyond talented. Jeff will do a good job showing his work off in the magazine; wait and see. Have you seen any of his photography, Mama? He's outstanding."

"I've not; I'll have to google him later." I reached for her and kissed her. Then, I turned to go.

"Wait, Mama! You haven't seen what Louie created for me for the shower. Look at this and tell me what you think?"

As Isabella held up the simple jumpsuit in a rosy pink with a coral pattern across it, I smiled at its Native American Indian colors and designs. I knew without a doubt that the turquoise necklace and earrings I'd bought as a gift for Isabella would be the perfect accessories for it.

"Stunning. Beautiful, just like you, my sweet Little One."

"Oh, Mama, I'm so excited! I can't believe I'll be Mrs. Samuel Brooks in just a few days!"

I stopped dead at hearing what she'd said. It meant that she would no longer be Isabella Bennett but Isabella Brooks. I'd forgotten that her name would change with her marriage, making me realize that Isabella would no longer be my daughter but Sammy's wife.

My eyes welled. "Where has the time gone? It seems like yesterday that you were that scared little girl at my front door. I'm so happy that you came into my life, Isabella. Thank you for being my daughter."

"Oh, Mama, I'll always be your daughter. That will never change."

"I know, sweetheart and I'll always be your mother." After a moment, I laughingly amended, "One of your mothers, that is."

"The best mother anyone could ask for, you mean."

I smiled as we reached for each other and hugged.

# CHAPTER 23

I t was so good to have Mike back with us again. All welcomed his calm demeanor and his loving personality around the family. On several occasions, Sammy had attested that Mike's behavior on the job as a detective was entirely different. I could see where his tall, toned physique alone commanded attention and would lead anyone to believe it'd be best not to cross him.

I'd gotten so used to Mike's softer side that after I'd told him about Harry's shenanigans, he startled me when he rose from his chair and began to pace the room.

"Damn it! What is Angela thinking? Doesn't she know better than to get mixed up with the likes of Harry? What does Miguel say?"

"I asked her if she'd spoken to her father yet, and she said no, but she would."

"Good."

"I'm bringing this all up because Angela asked Isabella if Harry could attend the wedding."

"What did she say?"

"I don't think she's decided yet."

Mike shook his head. "Knowing Isabella, she won't want to hurt Angela's feelings and say yes."

"I wouldn't put my money on it. Isabella doesn't like Harry at all."

"Should we say something to her about what we think?" Mike asked.

I shook my head. "No, not unless she asks us. It's her decision."

"Okay, you're the boss on that one," he said before kissing me. "I'm going to run on down and see Coyote. I'll be back."

I returned to sipping my coffee. Mike had a great relationship with Coyote and Miguel. They had become close, and each stepped into the father role to any of the kids when necessary. The kids were accepting of that when circumstances required it.

And Cal had played his part in all our relationships by becoming the great wise Grandfather. Cal had always had a creative mind and a good business sense. He'd been the one to help guide Miguel in setting up his own landscaping business. I smiled. We'd ended up like one big family, and I took a great deal of comfort in that, especially since my family growing up had been so small—only my grandmother and me.

Jack came out to the deck where I was sitting. "Mama?"

"Yes, sweetie, what is it?"

"Something bad is going to happen. I can feel it," he said with worry crossing his brow.

"Did you have a vision?"

"No, it's just a feeling this time. I don't like it, Mama."

"Well, I understand. It's not always easy to sense things before they happen. The only thing you can do is to stay calm and ask your "heaven" father to help you if there is anything you should be doing."

"I know."

"Come here, Jack," I said, holding my arm wide. As he stepped near me, I pulled him to me. "I love you, kiddo."

"I know that, Mama."

"Try not to worry. Things have a way of working out the way they're supposed to, right?"

"Yes," he sighed.

"How about I fix you a nice breakfast?"

"Eggs and bacon, too?" he asked hopefully.

"Deal." That wasn't the first time Jack had come to me with his prophetic feelings and visions. I didn't want to dwell on what he'd said, but I, too, felt trouble was close by, waiting for the "right" time to appear.

Isabella peeked out the door at us as Sweet Pea raced to her. "Good morning, you two!"

"Morning, Bella. Mama's making breakfast. Eggs and bacon!"

"Count me in!" she laughed.

I rose and patted Jack's head as I went inside. "Your face is flushed, Isabella. Are you feeling okay?"

"Just excited. Sammy gets in today," she grinned with sparkling eyes.

"I understand. It's nice to have your man with you," I laughed. "I know it is for me."

"Mama, I need your advice," Isabella said.

"Okay. Talk to me while I get the bacon started."

"I've decided to let Harry come to the wedding. Do you think I'm doing the right thing?"

I stopped and looked at her worried face. "I know that you don't want to disappoint Angela. You also know that Harry is a loose cannon. If you want to go ahead with it, I'd suggest you talk to Mike and the other fathers and ask them to keep an eye on Harry to nip any disruption in the bud."

Her face brightened. "That's a good idea."

"Tomorrow is the shower. Have you talked to Nica? Is Jeff here yet?"

Isabella's face split into a wide smile. "Yes, he came two days ago. He's driving Nica nuts because he wants to spend all his time with her."

I chuckled. "There are worst things than that."

"I think Nica's smitten with him, but you know her; she won't admit it."

"It's going to take quite a guy to corral her, that's for sure," I said.

"I agree," Isabella laughed.

I turned back to the pan of frying bacon. "Better tell Jack, the bacon is just about done."

# CHAPTER 24

A s I stood before the mirror scrutinizing Louie's designer outfit I wore, Mike stepped into the bedroom. His eyes lit up upon seeing me, and he walked toward me. He stood behind me and leaned his head down beside mine, admiring me through the mirror's reflection.

"I don't know how you do it, but you get more beautiful each day. I'm a lucky man."

"You're not so bad yourself, handsome."

He stood up straighter, pulled his shirt down, and puffed his chest out teasingly. "Really?"

I laughed. "Don't let it go to your head, mister."

He reached over and put his hand behind my head to pull me closer for a kiss. I squealed and tried to push him away. "My hair! You're crushing my hair!"

He laughed. "You sound like a little kid squealing like that."

I laughed, too, caught up in the silliness.

"Hey, what's going on?" asked Isabella, who'd come to the doorway. Jack pushed past her and raced in with Sweet Pea at his heels.

"What's the matter?" asked Jack.

"Mama and I were being silly," Mike said.

"Oh," Jack said, hunching his shoulders in boredom.

"Hey, buddy, what do you say? Shall we go out to lunch while the ladies of the house go to Isabella's shower?"

"Yeah! Let's go!" replied Jack.

"It's all about food with you, Jack. All someone has to do to win your heart is be a great cook," teased Isabella.

I winked at Isabella, smiling at Jack and shaking her head.

He laughed. "Yup."

"Come inside, Isabella, so we can see the outfit Louie designed for you to wear to the shower." Playfully, she swept into the room and twirled around with her arms spread wide. The jumpsuit fit her like another skin without being overdone. She looked beautiful.

"Can you believe it's come to this, Mike? Our little girl getting married?"

Mike stepped back to me and put his arm around my shoulders, pulling me close. "Your mother and I are so proud of you and the beautiful woman you've become, Isabella. Even though you'll be a married woman, you'll always be that special little girl to us that we love so much."

Mike bit back more words. For a tough guy, he got very emotional about how much he loved his family, and he was struggling not to tear up. We were quiet while we considered what Mike had said until Jack broke in, "Ready for lunch, Daddy?"

Isabella and I went to pick up Virginia and Maggie.

\*\*\*

When we arrived at Karen's house, guests were already there. It was a happy occasion, suggested by the noise and laughter reaching us as we walked inside. The ladies were sipping punch and chatting with each other, sharing their summer events. I looked around to see who was there. Knowing a photographer was going to be there, some of the women were a bit overdressed. And I smiled at that as I searched for Jeff. I wanted to ensure he took a picture of Maria and me as Isabella's two mothers. When I caught a pair of blue eyes behind dark-rimmed glasses looking my way, I smiled and waved. He did the same before coming my way.

Isabella had barely gotten inside the front door before she was surrounded by women wanting to see the sizeable two-karat diamond engagement ring she now wore. They oohed over her jumpsuit and insisted on her turning around so they could see all of it. Jeff began clicking away, taking one shot after another. I bit back a smile as I watched Isabella struggle to hide her discomfort at all the attention she was receiving. She hated anyone fussing over her. The idea of Jeff photographing her was a high price for her to pay for Louie's designs. But she'd do it with grace. That's who she was.

Later, as Isabella opened gifts, Angela and Nica sat next to her. Nica folded the wrappings into a neat pile while Angela took the ribbons and put them through a paper plate to make it look like a wedding bouquet. The gifts were lovely and thoughtful. But the gift that got the most attention was the one Grandmother had made for Isabella. It was a round silver disc with a raised profile of an Indian woman in relief and tucked into her neckline was the head of a female child. Small Turquoise and Coral stones were inlaid around it. It was beautifully made—not the least bit commercial—and exquisite. Knowing its significance, I could see that Isabella was stunned.

When dessert was passed out later, I overheard one of the ladies mention the rash of burglaries in town. She worried about the city becoming too large with all the new people who'd moved to Santa Fe and how things were changing.

Another woman joined in. "I ran into a group of young men while shopping. They blocked my pathway into the Chic Boutique, and when I asked them to please move, they were rude. They asked me what I wanted to buy inside. Can you imagine?"

"I don't know what our world is coming to," lamented the woman beside her.

I looked across the room to meet Angela's gaze. She'd been listening to the women talk, and when she saw me, she blushed and turned away. A vision of Harry came to mind when he'd done something similar. I sure hoped Angela would end that relationship soon.

Jeff was a darling during the entire shower, waiting patiently in the background for the right moment to take pictures. He followed Nica with his eyes as she acted as part hostess with Karen, checking on refills for the guests. Yes, he was smitten with her. There was no denying that.

The wedding was taking place in 48 hours. Isabella had gotten her way in not wanting a bachelorette party. As it was, she was happy to have the shower over and done.

Sammy was going out with his buddies tonight, and the girls and Jeff would meet up with them later. Having it tonight would give them plenty of time to regroup before the wedding.

Thanking them for attending the shower, Isabella and I stayed until the last person had gone. Jeff had promised to send a photo of the group picture to everyone. In it, he'd posed us in positions so that it looked more casual and not so arranged, and we all were curious to see how it turned out.

I joined Karen and Grandmother with a small glass of wine as I waited for Isabella to finish packing the car and make last-minute arrangements with Nica, Angela, and Jeff to meet later. It had been a beautiful shower, and I was grateful to Karen for hosting it. I knew it meant a lot to Isabella.

Coyote looked exhausted when he returned with the boys. Their two boys were a handful. I caught Karen's eye, and she winked at me.

I rose and kissed Grandmother goodbye. "I love you, Grandmother—my mother."

"Blessings to you, my daughter."

# CHAPTER 25

A s soon as we arrived home, Jack was at the door to greet us, his overnight bag at his feet. "I'm ready, Mama! Grandfather is waiting for me."

Jack was going to spend the night at Cal and Virginia's place. That would allow Mike and me to spend time with my sister-friends and their husbands. Nancy and Steve had finally married after years of living together in Boise, Idaho. They were now the proud parents of two sets of twins under eight years old, and they didn't want to make their non-married living situation difficult for their four boys when they attended school. Being boys, they probably wouldn't care, but surprisingly, Steve insisted they marry. And they were a happy, rowdy family with lots of animals.

Susannah (a Probate and Estate lawyer) and Henry (a Real Estate lawyer) were highly successful in their joint law firm in Boston, Massachusetts. They'd made a name among their peers and were highly regarded in their community. They'd decided long ago not to have children of their own, but after seeing the rest of the sister-friends with children, they adopted a child through the Save a Child Foundation. Although they didn't see him often, they remained in touch with him over the Internet when possible since the internet in South America wasn't always reliable. They filled their lives with two adorable silky terrier pups, like Sweet Pea.

I was excited to see my sister-friends. Reflecting on all four of us, I realized how fortunate we had been. To date, no one was terminally ill, and our home lives were happy. Goosebumps came to me, and I brushed away their foreboding.

Romano and Randy would arrive in the morning with Mimi, leaving her boyfriend, Charles, behind to run Rosalie's restaurant. It would be a quick trip for all of them because they were flying back to Las Vegas the day after the wedding. Knowing he'd try to control everything regarding wardrobes and annoy everyone, Louie and his partner purposely chose not to attend the wedding. Louie said, "I'm leaving it up to the gods and Jeff."

Instead of walking Jack over to Cal and Virginia's condo, I drove him there. "Isabella, tell Mike I'll be right back."

"Okay, Mama."

"C'mon, Jack, I'll drop you off at Grandfather's place."

I kissed him goodbye and watched him walk to the door when I arrived. Cal came outside and joyfully greeted Jack, clapping him on the back. He blew me a kiss and waved goodbye. I smiled and blew a kiss back.

Meeting Cal had been one of the best happenings in my life … a magical moment. Isabella had called him her grandfather shortly after they'd first met when he'd pretended to be a chauffeur instead of the owner of Mike and Brian's best client. Cal was such a good man, and Isabella and Jack adored him. He'd become like a father to me, and I loved him with all my heart. Lately, I worried about him after his minor heart attack.

Pulling away, I felt I should check in at the boutique. I'd heard Angela and Isabella talking earlier about letting the more experienced saleslady handle closing up the store at night. I decided to drive to Chic Boutique to change the code for the alarm system. I'd talked to Angela, who told me what she wanted the new code to be. As I drew closer to the store, goosebumps covered my body. Something didn't feel right ... something was off. I pulled into the back of the store to park instead of out front.

Something was up as I noticed the back door was not completely closed. I quietly pushed it open enough to squeeze through and stepped inside. I stopped when I heard the frantic plea, "Please, don't hurt me. You can take the money; just don't hurt me."

I reached inside my pocket for my phone and realized I'd left it in my purse in the car. I had to make a move if I didn't want the saleslady to get hurt. I carefully picked up one of the extra metal bars that fit into a display and advanced. I peeked around the corner and saw a man with his back to me wearing a full-headed ski mask looming over the terrified sales girl. Without thought, I raced forward and lifted my arm to whack him over the head. I felt movement behind me, and I found myself falling. Everything went black.

When I came to, a policeman stood over me. "She's coming around."

"What happened?" I asked as pain roared through my head.

"We got a phone call that there was a robbery here."

I sat up and looked around. The sales lady was crying and wiping her eyes and runny nose with her hand. Another policeman was handing her a tissue.

"Are you okay?" I asked her as I rose with the help of the policeman. I felt light-headed and clung to the policeman, fighting my dizziness.

She nodded. "I think so."

"Did you guys catch them?" I asked the police officers.

"I'm afraid not, Miss," said the older one.

"How much did they take?" I asked the saleslady.

"You disrupted them, so they only took the cash—about $1,000."

"Did you recognize them?"

She shook her head slowly back and forth. "They were young, though. Nervous and not experienced."

"Well, that's something. It sounds like the same burglaries as the others, then."

"I called Angela. She's on her way here," the saleslady said.

"Good," I said.

The police officers checked the back door to make sure the lock hadn't been broken. Miguel came with Angela to the store, and when he'd checked out the cameras he'd installed, the one aimed at the cash register area had been moved—turned away so that all it was recording was the ceiling. The cameras were small and well-hidden enough to be hard to find unless you knew the locations. Who knew about them besides Miguel, the girls, Karen, Maria, and me?

An hour later, I left the store. It was time to get Mike involved. We needed to catch the thieves at their own game. We just had to get through the wedding first.

# CHAPTER 26

**E**ven though my head pounded from where the thief had hit me, I was looking forward to Isabella's and Sammy's wedding ceremony at the Pueblo. It was such a simple, happy affair that everything flowed without tension.

Jeff was great, fitting in like family, as he photographed the ceremony, ensuring Louie's designs were shown off in the best light. Unsurprisingly, he seemed to be taking more pictures of Nica than anyone else, even the bride. I wondered if anything would develop between them. I hoped so because I liked Jeff.

The reception at the Eldorado Resort Hotel and Spa was filled with much laughter and chatter, and as I looked around, I felt so lucky to have my sister-friends and loved ones with us. I would have been heartbroken not to have them here. Soon, we heard silverware clanking against glasses—it was time for the groom to give his toast. I was curious to know what Sammy would say. He often appeared somewhat blasé, while he was surprisingly poetic when expressing himself at other times.

When Sammy stood, all eyes were drawn to his overwhelming beauty. He was far more handsome than any human being had a right to be. He turned to Isabella and raised his glass.

"I salute you, my wife, my life. Some things go beyond time and space. When I first saw you, I recognized you as my special gift in this lifetime. I knew then that our past wish had been granted, and we were allowed to become man and wife again. Some loves never die, never end. I claim you as my true love and give you my heart forevermore. I love you, Isabella."

Silence filled the room, and eyes filled with tears as his words resounded in our minds and hearts. Then, someone in the back yelled, "Hear, hear."

Cheers were hollered and whooped as we stood as one and raised our glasses in a toast to honor the beautiful couple.

I could see Sammy's speech had moved Isabella. She mouthed, "I love you, too," as he bent to kiss her. Maggie reached across the table and squeezed my hand. She didn't need to say anything because I knew exactly how she felt. I squeezed her hand hard and smiled at her. David wiped tears away and then grinned. "That boy knows how to give a toast, alright!"

We laughed, and as the music began to play, Mike held out his hand to guide me onto the dance floor. "Come, my queen. They're playing our song."

It was indeed one of our favorite songs. As we danced close together, Mike lowered his head and softly sang the lyrics into my ear. My heart melted. I sure loved that man.

Rosa, Jack, and Sarah were the youngest in attendance and got along well. They made up a threesome who did many things together, even though Rosa was a few years older.

Maria's three boys were growing up fast. Armando, the oldest and a teenager, stayed close to his father's side. He was now quite grown up and somewhat reserved, doing office work for his father's landscaping business. Ricardo was a bit more social than his brother and loved being outside doing labor work for his father's company. "Little Miguel" was the pistol of the group, finding fun and pleasure in everything he did—teasing Jack, Sarah, and Rosa mercilessly. He was an excellent salesman working with his father's customers. With the three boys assisting him, Miguel was doing exceptionally well in his business. He'd already earned a reputation for being honest and thorough.

When the tempo of the music changed, I watched as little Miguel asked Sarah to dance. At first, I thought she would reject him, but she rose to the occasion and took his hand. Jack saw this and immediately asked Rosa to dance. When the four of them were out on the floor dancing in abandonment, my heart sang to see them. I loved their spontaneity and their closeness.

Angela and Harry came onto the dance floor. He was leaning down and spitting words at her, and she continued shaking her head no. He was angry, and it showed. He grabbed her hand and yanked her off the dance floor, passing by us and heading for the door. She pulled back, and we could hear her, "No, Harry, I'm not going with you."

"If you don't go with me now, we're through. Do you hear me?"

She nodded, and her eyes filled.

Miguel stepped around his daughter, surprising them both, and asked in a low voice, "Is there a problem here?"

Angela flushed bright red. "No, Dad, Harry's just leaving."

Miguel stepped closer to Harry and whispered something in his ear.

Harry's face paled. "I'm going, but you haven't seen the last of me, Angie."

It was hard to miss what was going on. As Harry headed out, Angela raced to the Ladies' room in tears. Nica followed her.

As the night ended, I said goodbye to all the beautiful people who had come all this way to attend the wedding. Maggie and David would stay for another few days, but the rest would fly out early tomorrow morning. Even Isabella and Sammy were leaving then, headed off to the Greek Islands for their honeymoon.

I kissed Grandmother on the cheek. "Goodnight, my mother."

"Blessings, my daughter," she replied, taking hold of Angel's extended arm.

Coyote's sister Angel was a good daughter to Grandmother, and I honored her for that. As the mother of Nica, she was always somewhat distant to her, but I hadn't heard the true story of what'd made her act that way. Nica always claimed that it had been Grandmother who had raised her, not her mother.

Angela, Nica, and Jeff came to say goodnight, along with Sammy's friends who'd come for the wedding. "Where are you all off to?" I asked Nica.

"We're going to the Starlight Club for more dancing and karaoke. Don't worry. We'll be careful."

Mike came to my side. "No driving, hear? Call a cab or call me if need be."

"Okay, Uncle Mike," Nica said. "Will do."

Mike took my hand and led me to where Sammy and Isabella stood, waiting for us before heading to the bridal suite.

# CHAPTER 27

## Present Time

I woke up in pain. Going to High Tea with Isabella and Joslin yesterday caused my foot to swell from not raising my leg as I was supposed to. My new knee replacement was aching since it was not completely healed, and I rose to stretch my leg.

When I came back to bed, Mike reached out for me. "Can't sleep?"

"I can't stop thinking about the past."

"I hope you're thinking about the good parts," he chuckled.

"I guess not. I recalled Angela's boyfriend, Harry, of all things. What a mess that was!"

"One hard lesson learned there," he added. "Did you take a pain pill so that you can sleep?"

"Yes, and you need to go back to sleep, too. I know you have a busy day tomorrow."

"Yes, Brian is flying in for a few days."

"His room is all set. Go back to sleep, Mike. I'm going to be fine."

He kissed my forehead and turned away from me. As I lay there, it did not take long before Mike snored away. I wished getting to sleep was that easy for me. I closed my eyes, and my thoughts returned to what happened after Isabella's wedding …

\*\*\*

"Don't worry, Uncle Mike. We promise not to drive," Nica had said.

Jeff had stepped closer to shake Mike's hand. "No worry, sir, I've got this."

After Mike and I said goodbye to Isabella and Sammy, we headed home with Jack to get a good night's sleep. The wedding was an enormous success, and I couldn't have been more pleased.

When the home telephone rang, Mike stirred but didn't wake. I could see I'd have to answer it.

"Hello?"

"Rosie, I need to talk to Mike," Coyote said in a rush.

"What's wrong?"

"The police have just arrested Harry and some other boys for burglary. Angela was with them."

"Angela? Why would she be with them?"

"That's what we need to find out. I want Mike to be here to help Miguel. You know his temper."

"Here's Mike now," I said, handing the phone over to him. "Coyote," I mouthed.

"Hey, Coyote, what's up?" Mike listened as Coyote explained the problem. "Okay, I'll head to the police station right now."

Mike was upset. "What's the matter with that girl that she won't stay away from that fool? He's nothing but trouble." Mike hurriedly pulled on the same dungarees he'd worn yesterday and a clean tee shirt.

"Let me know what's happening, okay? I'll worry until I hear from you," I called after him as he raced out the door.

I went back to bed even though I knew sleeping would be impossible. I wondered if I should try to reach Nica. Instead of calling her, I texted her to see if she was awake. A minute or two later, I heard the ping on my phone, letting me know I had a message. It was Nica telling me to call her.

"Nica, Angela is in trouble. What happened last night?"

"Rosie, it was a mess. Harry and his buddies found us at the bar and insisted on joining us. Harry thought Jeff was with Angela, and he went berserk. Jeff was finally able to straighten things out by telling Harry that he was with me. Later, when Harry watched Angela laughing and having fun with us, he grabbed her and pulled her off the stool where she was sitting. 'You're coming with me!' he ordered. Angela protested. 'No, Harry, it's late, and I need to get home,' she told him. Harry got even angrier. 'I don't trust Four Eyes to do that. I'm going to be the one taking you home, understand?'"

"What happened next?" I asked.

"You know how much I hate that guy, Auntie Rose, and I don't trust him. So, I got up and grabbed Angela's arm, pulling her away from Harry. I told him, 'She's staying with me.' Of course, that infuriated him, and he started to make an even bigger scene. Noticing that everyone was watching us, Angela turned to me. 'Just let me go with Harry. He can drop me off at home.' That's all I know," she sighed.

When I remained silent, Nica asked, "Is there more to the story, Auntie Rose?"

After I told her about Angela being arrested, she said, "I know she wouldn't be involved in a burglary. Harry must have set her up."

"I think so too, Nica. Now we need to prove it."

We said our goodbyes, and I promised to get back to her as soon as I heard anything from Mike. I leaned back against the pillows, lost in thought. Soon, I listened to the patter of feet as Jack and Sweet Pea came my way.

"What's the matter, Mama?" asked Jack.

"There's a problem that Daddy has to help get straightened out."

"Is it about Angela?" he asked.

Amazed at his knowledge, I didn't say anything—just nodded.

"I'm not surprised," he said in a grownup voice. "C'mon, Sweet Pea, I'll let you out."

I sat there thinking about how we would prove Angela's innocence. Intuitively, I knew Harry and his buddies would gang up on her, and she'd be outnumbered, unable to defend herself against what they said. They'd create enough doubt about her innocence that those in charge wouldn't readily dismiss her part in it. Not being careful about who you choose to have in your life was a hard lesson that Angela needed to learn.

Knowing Maria would be distraught, I decided to get showered, dressed, and head over to her house to see what I could do to help her out. I got out of bed and went into the kitchen to find Jack. He was sitting at the table eating some cereal and fruit. "Hurry up and finish eating, Jack, and quickly get dressed. We're going to go to Auntie Maria's house."

"Okay, Mama."

When we arrived, Maria was in tears, arguing with her sons. "All three of you need to go to work in the morning as you promised your father you'd do. There's nothing you can do here. I'll let you know as soon as I have an update, okay?"

"Hi, Auntie Rose and Jack," said Armando, the eldest son.

"Your mother is right. We'll let you know when anything changes," I said.

"I promise," confirmed Maria.

The boys shuffled out, and Jack entered the kitchen, where Rosa made Mexican coffee for us. Maria looked at me, "What a mess! How is this going to end, Rosie?"

I was quiet because I wasn't receiving any visions. "I don't know," I answered honestly.

"Harry's from a rich, white family, and Angela's family is Mexican. Is there any doubt about how it's going to go down?" Maria asked bitterly.

"Hopefully, it won't come to that. We need to let those thoughts go, and once we have the details of what took place, we can move ahead to clear Angela if it even gets that far."

"You're right," Maria whispered. "We need to keep our heads and not get ahead of ourselves."

The day dragged by, and it was six long hours before Mike and Miguel came through the door looking bedraggled and defeated. My heart flopped when Mike looked me in the eyes and shook his head in despair. Miguel walked past us and headed into his bedroom, where, in a manner of seconds, we could hear him sobbing in sadness and frustration. Maria left us to join him, and Mike went to find Jack. I left a note for Maria telling her to call us when they were ready to meet with us. Then, the three of us went home.

# CHAPTER 28

O nce home, Mike and I sat down to discuss Angela's situation. I couldn't believe that there was any question about her lack of involvement in all the robberies that had taken place. "Without proof, what are they accusing Angela of doing?" I asked, frustrated.

"Angela said that she begged Harry to drop her off at home, but he refused. He told her he wasn't ready to end the evening, and he kept driving around until she said she couldn't keep her eyes open and fell asleep. The next thing she knew, she heard shouting and footsteps running toward the car where she sat inside, alone. She locked the doors, and it was only when she saw police officers behind Harry and the other boys that she knew something terrible had happened. When the boys tried to get inside the car, she refused to let them in. The police officers caught up to the boys, and Harry went wild, cursing and telling her he'd get her back.

"Here's the thing, Rosie. Harry told the police that she was the one who came up with the idea of robbing the store in the first place. He said it was just fun and games with her … that she liked seeing how far they could go without getting caught."

"And the police believed Harry? You've got to be kidding!"

"His parents have already hired a fancy lawyer, and the other boys involved have told the police the same story as Harry's."

"It doesn't make sense, Mike! Angela would never do that."

"Of course not. You and I know that, but Harry's lawyer is pushing the whole Mexican thing and how all the illegal Mexicans here think they have a right to whatever they want."

"How much worse can this get?" I moaned as Mike's cell phone rang, and he picked it up.

Mike's face drained of color as he listened to the message. "I don't believe it! Let's meet at Miguel's house in 15 minutes. I want to be there when he hears the news, and I want the whole family there, including Karen and Nica. Cal and Virginia have company, so we'll fill them in later."

"What now?" I asked as worry pounded in my chest.

"The police found some of the stolen items hidden at the Chic Boutique." He paused, anger showing on his usually placid face. "Harry told them where to look."

"Harry told them? That's a setup, for sure. Don't the police understand that?" I asked in frustration.

"Calm down, Rosie. We'll get to the bottom of this, I promise. Call Virginia and Cal and see if Jack can stay with them while we go to Maria and Miguel's house."

After explaining Angela's situation as quickly as I could, Virginia said, "Of course, you can drop Jack off here. And Sweet Pea, too. We'd love that."

A wave of gratefulness washed over me. How insanely lucky we were to have Virginia and Cal in our life. Their kindness, generosity, and love had confirmed that, time after time. "Thanks so much, Virginia. That'd be a big help."

Of course, Jack was psyched to spend time with Grandfather, Virginia, Maggie, and David. Even Sweet Pea seemed excited as she hurried after Jack when we dropped them off. Then, with heavy hearts, we headed to Maria and Miguel's house.

Once inside, it was easy to see that Miguel had already heard the news. He'd passed the grieving stage of what had taken place and was now angry … at everyone. Coyote, Karen, and Nica were sitting on the couch. Chairs had been pulled around so that we would sit in a circle, and Miguel was in the center, spitting out expletives in response to something Karen had asked. After listening to a few words, Mike stood up next to Miguel. "Do you feel better now, Miguel?"

Miguel studied each one of us. Knowing how angry he could become, we sat tense and uncertain about how he would respond to Mike's question. Then Miguel relaxed his shoulders and chuckled with embarrassment. We all laughed with him, thankful for the release of tension and worry. Mike asked, "Coyote, where do we stand on this?"

"The only thing that's changed since this morning is the discovery of some of the stolen goods hidden at the

Chic Boutique. All of us here know that it has to be a setup by Harry. The policemen are questioning everyone at the store to see how he could have gotten inside without a key or set off the alarm to plant the goods."

Nica began to squirm in her seat, and her face reddened. "That might be my fault, Uncle Coyote. The other night, I wasn't aware that Harry was standing behind me when I punched in the alarm code. He could have gotten it then. I'm sorry I didn't mention it to anyone before this."

"Do you know anything about him having a key, Nica?" he asked.

Nica's face darkened. "Angela told me that she thought Harry might have taken the extra key we have hidden. When she asked Harry about it the other day, he became furious that she would even think he had it. But I think he did take it because we can't find it anywhere."

I reached for my cell phone. "If I can reach the locksmith and promise him extra money, maybe he'll agree to do an emergency call to change the locks at the boutique this afternoon."

"Good idea," Coyote said.

"Coyote?" Mike asked. "You said that there was only a fraction of the stolen goods found in the store. Where are the rest of them? If we find them, maybe that will lead us to the person in charge of all these burglaries."

We all nodded in agreement. "Any ideas, Rosie?" he asked as I rose from my seat to go into the kitchen and call the locksmith, which was less noisy.

"The police have already checked out his house, right, Coyote?"

"They didn't find a thing," he confirmed.

"Sorry, Mike, nothing is coming to me," I stated sadly. "Nica? Is Jeff still here?"

She nodded. "Why?"

"It might not be bad for you two to go bar-hopping tonight and see what the talk is around town. I wouldn't want you to go by yourself, though."

"That sounds like an excellent idea. I'll ask him."

A knock came at the door, and Maria went to see who it was. I followed behind her. Cal clutched an 8" x 10" white piece of paper. He kissed Maria and then handed her the document to see. I saw what it said. "Go home, Mexicans. You're not wanted here."

A sad expression crossed Maria's face. Cal leaned toward her and whispered, "I found this taped to your front door. I don't think showing this to Miguel will do any good. I'll put it in my pocket and give it to Coyote later, okay?"

Maria nodded her head. "Yes, I agree. Come on in, Grandfather."

He stopped and kissed me before he trailed Maria inside. I put my hand on his arm, making him hesitate. "I'm glad you're here, Grandfather."

Grandfather had a calming way about him, always welcomed in a time of crisis. He clapped Miguel on the shoulder as he came to sit near him. After sitting, he said, "So, Coyote, why don't you catch me up on what's going on with our girl, Angela."

It was not lost on us why Cal had asked Coyote the question, not Miguel. It was clear that Miguel was having difficulty controlling his frustration and anger at the situation. However, he seemed to relax after Cal announced, "My lawyer is ready to represent Angela if it comes to that, Miguel and Maria. So, don't worry about that end of things. Let's see what we can do about catching Harry at his blame game, shall we?"

All the pawn shops in Santa Fe and the surrounding areas of Albuquerque had been warned and were looking out for the stolen items. Mike and Cal agreed to visit them the next day to make sure nothing had slipped by the pawnshop owners and the stolen items were in their store. We bantered about different scenarios, but it always returned to finding the rest of the stolen objects.

We ended the afternoon by agreeing to keep in touch with one another. Angela was to spend the night in jail until she had a hearing with the judge, who was out of town and due back tomorrow. The thought of her there alone saddened us all, and our eyes filled with sorrow.

# CHAPTER 29

**B**y the time Mike and I ended up at Cal and Virginia's condo, we were exhausted from worry and upset. I frowned in concern when I saw Sweet Pea slip and lose her footing when she greeted us. I picked her up and was amazed that she seemed so light like she'd lost some weight. Sweet Pea was aging. I kissed her furry cheek and carried her inside, holding her tightly. I greeted Maggie and David. They'd be flying back to Las Vegas the day after tomorrow.

It was nice for the six adults to sit together and relax with a cocktail while Jack quietly played a video game on the TV. Cal, Mike, and I began to update the others about what was happening with Angela.

"I can't believe they're making her spend the night in jail!" exclaimed Virginia.

"I agree," said Maggie. "That doesn't seem right. Were the other people involved going to spend the night in jail too, or is it just Angela?"

I shrugged, and Mike said, "Harry's lawyer was fighting that when I left the station earlier, so who knows?"

"I'll be happy when Harry gets payback for trying to get Angela involved in all he's been doing!" protested Virginia. "I don't want him to get away with it just because he has a fancy lawyer."

"Well, all you have to do is discover where he's hidden the rest of the stolen property," I said disbelievingly, patting her hand.

"You mean if all the stolen items can be found and tied back to Harry, Angela will be free from it all?" Maggie asked.

"Exactly. It's that simple, yet, we have no idea where it could be hidden since the police have already searched Harry's house, and they can't find anything," I sighed.

"It has to be somewhere. The question is, where?" David said.

"Mama?" Jack said as he turned to face us.

"Yes, sweetheart, what is it?"

"What are you looking for?"

"All the stolen items that were taken in the recent robberies around town," I answered.

"Do you mean all that stuff that Harry has stolen?"

"Yes. Why?"

Jack remained quiet.

"Do you know where it is?" I asked.

Never one to expand his words, he replied, "Yup,"

Astonished, we all stared at him until Mike asked, "Where is it, Jack?"

"It's in the doghouse," he said casually.

"If I remember correctly, Harry doesn't have a dog because he's allergic to them. Are you sure, Jack?" I asked.

"Yup, I'm sure. It's in the doghouse."

"How do you know that, Jack?" asked Maggie.

"When I heard you were talking about it, the answer came to me, and the voice is never wrong," he stated as a simple fact.

We looked at each other in amazement. Finally, Mike excused himself to call Coyote. For nearly an hour, we waited on pins and needles until we heard Mike's phone ring. We watched his face crumble with the news. "There's no doghouse on Harry's property. Sorry, Jack, I guess the voice was wrong this time."

Jack frowned. "No, Daddy, the voice is right. All that stuff is in the doghouse."

Mike was still talking to Coyote when an idea came to me. "Ask Coyote if there is a shed on the property."

After asking him, Mike smiled and nodded. "Although the police have already gone over it once, he says he'll check it out himself.' He turned back to the phone, "Call us back as soon as you can, okay?"

We waited once more for Mike's phone to ring. Twenty minutes later, we all leaned forward in our seats as we watched Mike pick up his phone. As he listened to what was being said, he smiled. With thumbs up, he nodded to us. "Thanks for getting back to us so quickly, Coyote. Yes, I'll tell him."

"What happened?" I asked.

"Coyote asked Harry's father for the key to the shed, who hollered to Harry's mother to give him the keys to the doghouse! It's a family joke that whoever misbehaves is threatened with being sent to the doghouse. Since there is no real doghouse, the shed became it."

161

"So, Jack, you were right all along," I said as he came to my side, and I hugged him.

"Yup," he said with a smile.

"Uncle Coyote said to tell you that you have a job with him whenever you're ready," Mike said, and we all laughed.

# CHAPTER 30

## Present Time

**M**y knee began to throb, and I turned on my other side to relax my leg. Remembering back to that time, I chuckled at the vision of us toasting Jack for helping Coyote discover where Harry had stored the stolen items. We'd felt vindicated that Harry would now suffer the consequences for his wrongdoing without dragging Angela further down. We knew that one didn't entirely escape the accusations once accused of something without leaving some doubt behind. So, from that point on, Angela would have to learn to hold her head high with the thought that her only wrongdoing had been her choice of a boyfriend.

With that last idea in mind, I closed my eyes and let sleep invade my space, happy to succumb to the void of darkness.

I awoke in a daze in the morning since I hadn't slept well because of the pain in my knee. Mike had quietly slipped out early to pick up Brian at the Albuquerque airport. Brian had taken the last flight out of Boston, landing in New Mexico around six o'clock this morning.

I automatically reached out for Sweet Pea, who usually would be by my side after Mike vacated the bed. I wiped away my tears at the thought of her passing and my selfishness in not wanting her to leave me. It took me several seconds to realize that many years had passed since her death. I'd been devastated when we'd had to put her to sleep. My heart flopped at the void I still felt without her. In the end, she'd steadily looked me in the eye, and it had been as if she'd spoken, telling me she loved me and to please let her go—that her time was up.

A few years after Sweet Pea had passed, I awoke one morning with a certain heaviness, knowing that days were numbered for Grandmother. I rolled over onto my back. I'd seen her passing, and I didn't know how I would be able to let her leave. But then again, what choice does any of us have when death comes calling?

It was still difficult to remember that time for several reasons...

\*\*\*

Once again, we'd returned to Santa Fe for the summer when Jack was seventeen. He'd grown to nearly six feet and filled out. Looking very much like a jock, Jack surprised most people when he said he wasn't interested in playing regulated sports. Even though many of his friends had summer jobs in Las Vegas, Jack had used his summer to volunteer on the Indian reservation where Nica and Karen were involved.

Jack and Nica had become close through their artwork, with Nica serving as his mentor. Nica was now a well-renowned artist, enjoying popularity as the Navajo's premier artist. Interestingly enough, Jeff was still in the picture and had been responsible for getting her artwork noticed in the first place. Although Nica and Jeff had never married, they might well have. Theirs was a wonderful but bizarre long-distant relationship. I wasn't going to knock it, though, since both of them were happy with it, which was all that mattered.

As much as I knew Jack was happy to do his volunteer work, I was well aware that part of his enthusiasm was because Karen's daughter, Sarah, was also going to volunteer at the reservation for the summer. Even though Sarah had proclaimed many times that she and Jack would marry one day, it wouldn't be anytime soon. She was too busy flirting with the many boys who gathered around her, admiring her stunning beauty. Karen and Coyote weren't too happy about the situation, so they closely watched Sarah to ensure nothing got out of hand. Coyote wouldn't stand for it.

Jack appeared indifferent about Sarah's behavior, but I knew him well enough to know it bothered him to see her act so friendly to all the other boys who vied for her attention. So, he ignored her and left her alone. According to Karen, that didn't sit well with Sarah.

I, too, had my work cut out for me at that time since Isabella was staying in Las Vegas for most of the summer. I'd oversee the running of the safe house in Santa Fe that was part of the Trust that she and I had set up for Cal to honor his birth mother, who had been a victim of her addictions.

Isabella would spend time with her active six-year-old twin boys. They were involved in swimming lessons, T ball, and playing on the beginner soccer team. Isabella had her hands full to the point she often asked Mike or Jack to step in for her at one of the games when she got caught up in overtime work for the Trust or working with the police to help them psychically on a case.

Mike was now well into his 60s and thinking about retiring early now that Sammy worked with him in the Las Vegas agency. As it was, Mike could choose what assignments he was willing to take on himself and leave the rest to the others. No matter what he decided to do— retire or work part-time—he'd always have his hand in the business to ensure that all was as it should be. After all, no intelligent person in business completely ignores the running of his company—and most certainly not the financial end of it.

Sammy was a good influence on Mike because he was relaxed and laid back, most likely due to his psychic abilities, allowing him greater insight into their assignments. With Sammy able to take charge, and Patricia Newheart, the receptionist Mike had hired years ago, still there, the office ran smoothly without a great deal of stress.

Brian was flying into Santa Fe to discuss a business opportunity with Mike. A more prominent security firm was interested in buying out both their Boston and Las Vegas offices.

Brian was my age, nearly ten years younger than Mike, and it was odd to me that he wanted to accept the offer while Mike didn't.... instead of the other way around. That, alone, showed their different personalities.

I had dubbed Brian the nickname "Cowboy" because he was a player, unsettled, always looking for the next woman or the next thing of interest. He was a great guy—kind, intelligent, funny—and would be a great catch for any woman if he could commit to being with just one person. "I haven't found the right woman yet," he told me after I'd asked him if the day would ever come for him to settle down.

Brian liked the idea of the wealth that selling the businesses would provide, leaving him more freedom to do what he wanted.

On the other hand, Mike happily settled with his family, liked the challenge and contrast of unexpected happenings and challenges in his profession. The Boston and Las Vegas offices had grown and expanded, and Mike was content with how things were and didn't want things to change.

When Mike first learned of this offer, he'd asked me what I thought about it. "I think you and Brian should get together and take your time to discuss all the pluses and minuses of accepting this offer. There are many things to consider. You both like being your own boss and if the new company wants you to stay on, are you willing to work for someone else? You've also talked about working part-time; what effect will that have on Brian, Sammy, and the others? Brian is younger than you, so he might not be in the same situation as you. I think that the two of you have a lot to discuss."

"Yes, I agree. There's a lot of new construction in Las Vegas and not so much in Boston. Maybe we should sell just the Boston office," he said.

I shrugged my shoulders. "I'll support whatever decision you make. I'm glad that Brian is coming here to Santa Fe, which will give you more private time away from the office to discuss all your options, and maybe you can even play some golf to relax too."

"I like the way you think, woman!" he laughed. "Maybe Jack can join us for golf. I'll ask him."

"Why not?" I smiled at the idea of the two of them together. I loved seeing how close they were.

# CHAPTER 31

When I walked into the kitchen and saw Brian, I smiled. Lord, he was handsome! "Hi, Cowboy!" I said, calling him by the nickname I'd given him.

"Hi there, beautiful. Where's the kid?" he asked, good-naturedly referring to his Godson as "the kid." He eagerly stepped forward and gave me a big, brotherly hug.

"Jack should be getting up any time soon. Feel free to go and wake him if you want."

"Are you kidding? Not me! I know when to leave a sleeping dog lay," he laughed.

Jack could be cranky in the morning, and we all teased him about it. Mike and I let him sleep in if nothing was planned for the day. He usually was up by ten anyway, ready to jump into things by then.

"I'm heading up to see Grandmother. Why don't we plan to go out for dinner tonight; is that okay with you?" I asked.

"I'll make the dinner reservation for seven, okay?" Mike asked.

"Perfect," I said as I kissed him goodbye.

\*\*\*

Driving to Grandmother's house, I remembered my first time meeting her and how much she had influenced my life—all our lives. It was hard to imagine a more generous gift could have been given me than to have my mother from a previous life now in my life again. Add to that Isabella, my sister in that same life, becoming my daughter in this one. How does that happen? How lucky could anyone get?

Knowing that Grandmother didn't have much time left made me sad. I loved her with all my heart and soul. She was the one who had taken the place of my mother, who had died when I was just nine, and then my grandmother, who'd raised me from that point, dying at an early age when I'd been in my mid-20s. Even though my grandmother's spirit still came to me with loving messages, Grandmother had filled the vast void both women had left when they passed. And, sad to say, Grandmother would be the last to fill that position since I was past the age of adding another mother figure.

As I drove into the Tesuque Pueblo, my heart fluttered. It felt like coming home after a long time away, although I'd been here just a few months ago. I walked up the path to Grandmother's house and knocked on the door. Nica answered.

"Hi, Auntie Rose. I'm so glad that you're here. Grandmother has been impatiently waiting for you to arrive."

"That doesn't sound like her," I said, worried.

Nica chuckled. "Maybe it was me that was so impatient," she confessed.

"What's going on?"

"I don't like to leave Grandmother alone these days, even if she insists she's okay. Jeff is flying in late tomorrow, and I need to prepare him at the studio."

"No worries. Now that I'm here, I've got this covered."

"Angel will be home soon, and she'll take over," Nica said, referring to her mother.

"Okay, say goodbye to Grandmother and then scram, kiddo!"

"You're the best!"

I went into the kitchen to put on the kettle and placed some homemade cookies on a plate. I walked down the hallway to where Grandmother was sitting in her bedroom chair, looking out the window. When she heard me enter, she turned and smiled at me. "Hello, my daughter. I'm glad that you're here."

"I'm happy to see you, Grandmother—my mother. How are you feeling?"

"Like a bag of old bones," she chuckled.

"Well, that says a lot," I laughed. "I've put the kettle on for tea. Do you want to have it here or in the kitchen?"

"In the kitchen, please. It'll be good for me to get up and move about."

After helping to seat her, I poured our tea, remembering the time shortly after we'd first met when we'd brewed special tea that brought forth our memories of the life we'd shared. It was then that my little sister (Isabella) died of a snake bite, and both Grandmother and I have carried that guilt to the present time. I shivered at the thought.

"How are things with you, my daughter?" asked Grandmother. "Or should I call you Grandmother, too? Isabella sent me the latest pictures of her twins. They are very handsome."

I laughed. "It's hard to believe that I'm a grandmother, but whenever I'm around them, those boys make it easy for me to remember that I am. They are a handful, that's for sure."

Grandmother took another sip of her tea. "How is Virginia getting along without Cal?" she asked, worry crossing her face.

It was still hard for me to talk about Cal, who'd died of a heart attack less than a year ago. "She's doing okay. She still has the place here in Santa Fe, and with Cal leaving her a large inheritance, she can buy a house of her choosing wherever she wants. As you know, Cal left his house next to ours for Isabella. He said he always thought of it as her home ever since the first day we walked through it, and she announced that it was the perfect place for him." I smiled at the memory.

"It's nice that Virginia has financial freedom," Grandmother agreed.

"Did Isabella tell you what she has in mind regarding the cottage on her back property?"

Grandmother nodded. "Using it as an interim safe house is a good idea." She eyed me. "She needs to use her psychic ability to make sure that whoever she puts up there is the right fit, so there aren't problems."

"I agree, and Sammy will help to vet them, too," I added.

Content, we sat silently and sipped our tea until Grandmother asked, "What's on your mind, child?"

"I received a telephone call a few days ago asking me if I'd be interested in buying Tom Little Horse's ranch or, rather, I should say if the Trust would be interested. The current owner wants to sell it."

I sighed and unconsciously rubbed the diamond pendant hanging from a necklace I wore daily. It'd been made from the engagement ring Tom Little Horse had bought to give me before he was murdered. I wore it in his memory. Noting my actions, Grandmother asked, "My daughter? …"

"Even after all these years, Grandmother, I still feel his loss. It's comforting to know that he visits Jack now and then as my grandmother visits me."

Grandmother nodded. "It's hard to deny the sadness that has stayed in your spiritual energy since Tom Little Horse's death. I'm curious to know if you buy the ranch, will it eventually become Jack's?"

"I hadn't considered that. It would make perfect sense to keep it in the family, though, wouldn't it? You know how much Jack loves it here—the outdoors and everything to do with the Navajo Indians." I was quiet, alone in my thoughts. "I wonder what Mike would think about that."

Grandmother smiled. "You might be surprised."

"What do you mean, Grandmother?"

"Mike has been a wonderful father to Jack, and he's aware that there's value in Jack recognizing and honoring his heritage. Mike is selfless about that boy and only wants the best for his son, even if it means sharing him with Tom Little Horse's ghost."

I smiled at Grandmother's description of Mike. He was such a good man, and each day I spent with him only confirmed how lucky I was to have him in my life.

"Maybe Jack will want to spend some of the money Cal left him and invest in the ranch himself. He could rent it back to the Trust for a nominal fee. I'd have to check that out with our lawyer and accountant to see if that would work. But, of course, I'd have to talk to Jack and Mike first."

Grandmother nodded. "I still have that photo of Jack's great-grandfather and me. I think it's time to share that history with Jack. Will you bring him with you the next time you visit?"

"Of course, Grandmother."

"If you don't mind, I'll lie down now."

"Of course not. I'll help get you settled," I said, assisting her.

After tucking Grandmother into her bed, I sat in the bedroom chair beside her and closed my eyes. I fell into a deep sleep and dreamt. In my dream, I was running and getting nowhere, trying to reach Jack, whom I could see ahead of me. I sensed he was in danger, and I wanted to warn him. But he'd disappear whenever I thought I was a little closer to him. I kept trying to call out to him, but no sound would come. I began to cry tears of frustration. When I felt a hand on my shoulder, I realized real tears trailed down my cheeks.

"Rosie, wake up!" Karen said. "You're dreaming. Are you okay?"

"Oh, my God! My dream was so real. I think Jack is in trouble."

Alarmed, Karen asked, "What do you mean?"

"I need to go, Karen. Can you stay with Grandmother until Angel comes?"

"Wait, Rosie, where is Jack right now?"

I began to shake off my sleepy sluggishness. "I think Jack is playing golf with Mike and Brian."

"Why don't you call Mike and see?" she said in a calming tone, patting my shoulder.

"Of course, I don't know why I didn't think of that." I called Mike, and it immediately went to voicemail. Frustrated, I hung up without leaving a message. "I'll try Brian's number."

There was no answer there, either. My heart pounded when I left a message. "Brian, have Mike call me back. It's urgent."

Shortly after, my phone rang. It was Mike. "Is Jack with you?" I asked.

"No, he decided to meet some friends instead. He said he'd meet us for dinner, though. Why? What is it?"

"I think Jack is in trouble ...."

"What do you mean?" he asked, alarmed.

"I had a dream about him, Mike, and you know what that means."

"It's not always what it seems, though, right? Listen, calm down, and I'll see what I can do to track him down. I'll call you back as soon as I know anything. Don't worry. He's with friends."

I turned to Karen, "Mike said Jack was meeting some friends. Would that include Sarah?"

"I don't know. I'll call her."

I watched as Karen called Sarah, and I could tell by her expression that Sarah was not answering her phone. "I'm sorry; there's no answer, Rosie."

"I don't like this. Where would Jack be hanging out?" I asked. "Maybe he and Sarah are together."

"Here's Angel now. She'll watch Grandmother," Karen said. "Have you seen Sarah or Jack?" she asked Angel.

"Gosh, I haven't; is anything wrong?" she asked.

"I don't know. If you see either one, please have them call us immediately," Karen said.

"I sure will. I hope everything's all right."

Karen grabbed my arm. "C'mon, I'll drive."

Grandmother stirred. She reached out her hand to me, waving me over. "Be careful, daughter."

# CHAPTER 32

**K** aren called her boys and told them that if they saw or heard from either Sarah or Jack, call her immediately. As we headed for one of their friend's homes, I tried to slow my racing mind and take a deep breath. If I could settle into a mindless zone, I'd be able to use my psychic abilities to try to connect with Jack. I closed my eyes and tried to envision where he might be. Nothing clear came to me.

Karen pulled into the driveway of one of Sarah's friends. His mother was outside and came to the car. "Is Joey here?" Karen asked.

"No, he and the other kids were going into town. Why?"

Not wanting to upset Joey's mother, I touched Karen's arm to halt her. "We're looking for Sarah and Jack," I said.

"They're probably with the others," she announced, unconcerned.

"Okay, thanks. If you see them, please have them call us, okay?" Karen asked.

"Sure thing."

"Thanks, see you later," Karen said, backing out of the driveway to head to Santa Fe.

I closed my eyes and leaned back against the headrest. As we drove closer to town, I envisioned a group of kids huddled together, yelling and hollering at someone or something. "Let's go straight to Heritage Park. I think the kids might be there."

*** 

We pulled up next to the park and could nose into a parking spot where someone was leaving. People were drawn to the park, crossing before us to reach it. Karen and I got out of the car and followed. Noise and shouts became more evident the closer we got, and just like my vision, people circled something happening in the center, shouting out directives. My heart pounded as I pushed my way in through the crowd. I stopped still when I saw Jack in the center. He was crouched in a fighting mode and moving around another person whose back was to me. It wasn't until the other person moved enough and positioned himself differently that I could see his face. My heart fell when I recognized him. Although it had been several years since I'd seen him last, he still displayed an arrogance that was hard to deny. Karen came to stand beside me. When she recognized Jack's opponent, she looked at me in astonishment. Angela's former boyfriend, Harry, was eying Jack with anger. I began to move forward to stop the fight when I felt a hand on my shoulder holding me back. Mike stood beside me. "Let Jack work it out, Rosie."

I looked at Brian, who'd joined us. He nodded in agreement and said, "It's the right thing to do."

It became clear that I would take away his pride and confidence if I didn't let Jack handle this himself. It was with difficulty that I held my ground and didn't make a move. Looking around the crowd, I saw Sarah standing with her friends, looking upset. "You can take him, Jack. You can do it," she urged.

Jack didn't react to her words. He broke his stance and viewed the crowd only when he felt my presence. Seeing me staring at him, he hollered, "I've got this, Mom."

I nodded, and he turned back to face Harry, but it was too late. Harry had already made his move. He threw Jack to the ground, landing on him with his knees on either side of Jack's neck, choking him. Jack's face was getting red, and he struggled to breathe. I squeezed Mike's arm in distress.

"Roll over, Jack!" Mike yelled.

Jack began to squirm under Harry's hold, and it was with a strength most of us don't have that Jack could roll over so that he was now on top of Harry. Most people would say that Jack was super strong to do that, but I knew better. I'd seen Tom Little Horse's spiritual energy join Jack's, and that was how he'd had the power to overturn Harry's hold on him. I wrapped my arms around Mike, and he held me close. "Are you okay, Rosie? You look white as a sheet."

I nodded, unable to put into words what I'd seen. It was Harry's turn to be unable to breathe, and Mike hollered, "Let him go, Jack."

Jack rose and then held out his hand to help Harry up. Instead of obliging, Harry, furious at losing, pulled a knife from the sheath attached to his belt and lashed out at Jack, catching him in the leg. Jack jumped back with blood spilling onto the ground. Harry struggled to stand from his kneeling position, grinning. "Anybody else?" Upon seeing Mike step forward, he taunted, "Coming to save your Indian brat?"

Karen or Sarah must have called Coyote because he came forward, holding a pair of handcuffs. "That's enough, Harry, give me the knife. You're under arrest."

Mike handed the bandana he held in his hand to Jack. "Here, Jack, keep pressure on your wound with this. Come on; I'm taking you to the hospital so they can take a look at your leg."

"This ain't over yet, Indian boy," scoffed Harry, struggling against Coyote.

Jack lifted his head to stare into Harry's eyes. In a soft but steady voice, he replied, "Yes, I'm afraid it is, my friend. You're going to be in a car crash, and you're not going to make it. You'll never see the end of summer."

Harry's face lost all color. "Are you fuckin' casting an Injun spell on me?" he asked.

"No, I'm just telling you the truth," Jack said sadly.

As Mike and Jack turned away to leave, Sarah ran up to Jack. "I was so scared for you, Jack. Promise me that you'll never do that again!"

Jack blushed and laughed. "I'm not sure I can promise that, but I'll try, okay?"

Sarah smiled and punched him on his arm in a teasing way. "You'd better."

Karen and I stood to the side with our arms wrapped around each other. We grinned at the two of them. They were quite a pair.

# CHAPTER 33

S everal days later, Jack and I visited Grandmother, and he proudly showed off his stitches. "So, Jack, what did you learn?" she asked.

"Grandmother, it's more of what was confirmed for me. Some people carry enough disappointment in themselves to make others suffer for it. That is what Harry is all about."

"Your mother tells me that you told Harry about his death. Is that true?"

"Yes, Grandmother, I'm sorry. You have taught me better, but he caught me off guard."

"There's no reason to apologize this time. Things work out as they are meant to … maybe he will change his ways now."

"No, Grandmother, he won't," declared Jack, shutting out any doubt. "You wanted to show me something?"

"Yes, my child, here," she said, handing him the photo of herself and her husband. "Shall I tell you something about your grandfather and the history of your family? As you spend more time on the reservation, you'll hear stories, and I wanted you to hear about your family from me."

"Yes, Grandmother, I'd like to hear what you have to say," Jack answered, closely studying the photo. "I look just like him, don't I?"

"Yes, in some ways, as did your father. But before we begin, my daughter, why don't you pour us some of the tea Angel made for us?"

I handed each of them a mug of black tea that smelled deliciously fruity and then sat back on the sofa to listen to her story. I was just as curious as Jack to learn what she'd been like as a young woman, married to that handsome, stern man in the photo. And so, she began ...

\*\*\*

"I was a young girl, barely past fourteen years of age, when I first met him. His name was Black Crow, and he was the most handsome man I'd ever seen. He had dark, black eyes that saw everything. They were like yours, Jack, and your father's." She smiled at the remembrance of him. "He was 20 years old and stood over six feet tall. He was stern even then and exuded power and a charism seldom seen today. He was a modern-day warrior defending Indian rights, which earned him the respect of his elders and others."

"He'd heard I had the vision and one day, he came to see me, seeking advice. He wanted to know if he'd become chief of his pueblo, the one further north of here. There was no son to follow the chief there, and talk was going around that he would be voted in as the new one. So, I told him what I saw."

"What did you see, Grandmother?" Jack asked.

"I told him that he would become the chief of his pueblo, but after being in that position for a while, he would come to a fork in the road. He would have to choose how he wanted to live going forward. I refused to tell him then what else I'd seen because I knew how proud he was, and I didn't want to stir his anger."

"He thanked me and told my father he might want another reading again. Afterward, I told my father never to allow the man back, for I knew that Black Crow would ask for my hand in marriage if my father encouraged him. And I'd already seen his temper in my vision."

"How come you married him, then, Grandmother?" asked Jack.

"He was a man used to getting his way, and, back then, there was no thinking that a woman had a choice … that wasn't how things worked in those days. So, Black Crow got his way, and we were married shortly after I turned sixteen.

Grandmother was becoming tired and weak from telling her story, but she was determined to continue and spoke bluntly.

"I was the envy of all the women who saw him and relished the idea of laying with him. I was young and untrained in the ways to satisfy him enough to keep him to myself. In time, I became pregnant and reached the stage where I could not oblige his wishes, and he turned to other women to satisfy him. Those were difficult years. Black Crow struggled to make his words count in politics to ease some of the pain of government interference in tribal matters. And I was careworn with attending to a sickly son who seemed to attract any illness going around. I became too tired to care whether my husband wandered or not. Soon, I left him to go back to my father's house, and it was there that our son died."

"When word reached Black Crow, he came to me, begged my forgiveness, and pleaded with me to return home with him. I'd grown up during those first years and learned how to keep a man." Grandmother smiled, remembering. "We made love with an urgency to produce another child, and that is when we conceived Coyote's and Angel's father, Laughing Wolf. He was a big, beautiful, happy boy who loved to laugh. At the same time, unbeknownst to me, Black Crow had bedded another young girl, who gave birth to a squalling baby boy, Howling Wind, who was Tom Little Horse's father and your grandfather, Jack."

I caught Jack's eye, and a flash of understanding flowed between us. He seemed to take in the personal words of Grandmother, accepting that it was not unusual for older people to speak their truth without a filter.

"What happened next, Grandmother?" Jack asked.

"Howling Wind's mother began to drink. Often, when things were bad, he'd come to stay with us, making him and Laughing Wolf more like true blood brothers instead of half-brothers. Black Crow was busy in local politics staying close enough to home to enjoy his sons, and things were good for a while. We settled into a loving family until the boys reached the age of seven or so. Black Crow was pressured to extend his politicking nationally, and that is when the downfall began. He became ashamed of his family living in a poverty-stricken pueblo without the incentive to further their education more than what the pueblo could provide. Social drinking began to take over, and before too long, Black Crow was caught up in everything wrong with politics. And later, it was the disease of alcoholism that took him."

"Meantime, the boys without a male figure to mentor them grew up and acted out like many sons without fathers. They stayed close to home, living the simple Native American way of life under my jurisdiction. Then, without my approval, Black Crow encouraged them to sign up for the army at seventeen instead of waiting to be drafted. Laughing Wolf left a pregnant girlfriend behind, and on his first furlough, he returned home to greet his son, Coyote. And after his leave, he returned to the army, leaving his girlfriend pregnant with Angel.

"Meantime, Howling Wind married a girl in the pueblo and left her pregnant with Tom Little Horse when he returned to war. When their time was up, neither man re-enlisted but returned home broken and addicted to various drugs to help ease the terror and pain of the Viet Nam war. Plus, they had been affected by Agent Orange, which the government denied at the time. It was the only time I could recall that Black Crow was at odds with his colleagues in Washington and became enraged that the government wouldn't tell the public the truth. He died before the truth came out."

"This sounds so sad, Grandmother," Jack said.

"Yes. Those weren't happy times for many who returned from the war to find things so different—to return to the upheaval and righteousness of whether we should have been involved in the Vietnam War."

"So, what happened to them?" asked Jack.

"Like so many who returned home, things became too difficult for them to handle. They were angry, disheartened men who became ill with a disease no one knew how to treat, and alcohol became the solution to numbing their

185

pain. These two handsome young men lashed out at everyone and became physically abusive, taking out their anger on those they loved most. Those drugs brought them to the brink, and then suicide finally did them in," answered Grandmother as her eyes filled.

"Suicide?" questioned Jack.

Grandmother nodded. "I'm telling you this story not to make you sad but for you to remember who they were without the drugs and the effects of the war. They served their country, and it cost them their dignity to return home to be booed by others for their efforts, and eventually, it cost them their lives."

"What happened to my grandmother?" asked Jack.

"Your grandmother died of cancer, leaving Tom Little Horse behind at the early age of six. Howling Wind, your grandfather, died about ten years later," Grandmother said, "as did my husband, Black Crow. It was a sorrowful time."

Now caught up in the story, Jack asked, "So then, what happened to my father?"

"He had a hard life after his mother died, and he roamed the woods and meadows untethered; he was as wild as his father's name, Howling Wind. When he was tired of being alone, he'd come to stay with us for a while. Then, he'd leave again."

Grandmother took a deep breath, trying to regain her strength to continue. "Your father and Coyote were great pals growing up together, continually getting into trouble. Again, no male figure could take them in hand, and they ran wild. They fast became known as rowdy Indian troublemakers with their curious minds and spirit of adventure and caused me more than a few gray hairs. Luckily, each of them found someone later in their lives who helped turn them around. Coyote found a teacher mentor, and Tom Little Horse met a government agent to the Indians who became fascinated with your father's gift of words. He was the one who convinced your father to get involved in what was going on in Washington. Because of him, your father got into politics, although I think it was already part of his DNA."

"I want you to understand, Jack, that your father was a good man ... honorable. He was a survivor and believed in helping his kind. You come from a long line of men who became politically involved in doing what they could for the Native American Indians—even your grandfather, who was a soldier."

I've waited until now to share your father's last words with me, thinking you were old enough that they might mean something to you. Your mother hasn't heard them, but she will now too." Grandmother closed her eyes and drew a deep breath to take her back to that time.

*"One day, before your father was going to propose to your mother, he came to me to ask my blessing for the marriage since I was the only one left in the family. I knew how much he loved your mother, and she loved him too. As soon as he placed a kiss on my cheek, I had a vision of his death. But I never said a word about it. Instead, I told him that soon he'd have a son coming into this world. He was overjoyed."*

*"I'm not going to be like my father. I promise you, Grandmother, that I'll be a good father to my son," he said.*

*I told him, "Yes, you will love your son enough to share him."*

*"If you say so, Grandmother," is all he said.*

*Wanting him to leave his child a legacy, I asked, "What is the most important thing you'd teach your son?"*

*He didn't hesitate. "Two things, Grandmother. First, I'd tell him to find a good woman and love her without restraint, and second, I'd tell him to learn and respect the Indian ways, not allowing anyone to take anything more from the first people's land."*

Grandmother leaned back in her chair, seemingly exhausted. She barely spoke above a whisper as she continued. "I share your father's words with you, Jack, because I want you to learn what it was like for your father—where he came from and how strong he was to have survived all that he did. I want you to realize how far your father had come to present himself to Congress and fight for what he believed would benefit his ancestry. Your bloodline is strong, and with your "heaven" father and your "earth" father's guidance, you can make a difference in this world."

Jack was quiet, and Grandmother leaned forward and patted his hand. "Stay away from drugs, for they do you no favor. Yours is our generation of hope to change the world and fill it with love, understanding, and appreciation of each other. It is written in the stars. And I, among others, will be cheering you on."

Listening to Grandmother's words, Jack and I were overcome with emotion. It was easy to see that her words had profoundly affected Jack, and they had already set in motion some of his choices going forward—strengthening his destiny.

He leaned forward and cupped each side of Grandmother's face with his large hands, placing a kiss on each cheek. "Bless you, and thank you, Grandmother, for passing along my father's words to me. I will consider all that you've shared, and I will not disappoint you."

"My child, you could never disappoint me. Your journey and how you choose to live your life belong to you and no one else."

Having said what she wanted, Grandmother looked depleted, her body hunched in her chair. Worry filled me as I saw her condition, and I rose to collect Grandmother and return her to her bed.

"Come, Grandmother; I will help you get settled." After tucking her in, I sat on the edge of the bed. "Thank you, Grandmother, for sharing your words with Jack and me. They mean the world to us both."

As Jack and I rode home later, he was very subdued. "Are you okay, honey?"

He looked at me with tears in his eyes. "I've got to have the two best fathers anyone could have, don't I?"

"Yes, you do," I confirmed, wiping away tears of my own.

# CHAPTER 34

A few days later, I noticed a difference in Jack. He didn't seem himself. He'd become moody and almost didn't respond when I asked, "Is something wrong, Jack?"

"It's nothing, Mom," he said and walked away.

"Well, it doesn't seem like nothing to me. If you need to talk about anything, Jack, I'm right here," I called after him. I decided not to say anything to Mike since he and Brian were still discussing whether to sell the company, and he had a lot on his mind.

When I got into the car to head out to Grandmother's house, I noticed Jack's car was still in the driveway. I thought that he'd left for his volunteer work. Instead of my leaving, I went back inside to find him. He was sitting at his desk in his bedroom, working on his laptop. He was surprised to see me but said nothing.

"I want to know what's going on with you, Jack. I know you've been through a lot lately with what happened with Harry and all ...."

"Mom, it has nothing to do with that!"

"What then? You're beginning to worry me."

He looked at me, deciding whether to come clean or not. Finally, he spoke, "Since Sarah and I share the same bloodlines, does that mean we can never be married?"

I was so surprised to hear what he'd said that I couldn't find words for a moment. "Gosh, no, Jack. Of course, you can marry! Sharing your great-grandfather is too many generations back to be of concern. Is that why you have not been yourself? Thinking you couldn't marry Sarah?"

His face flushed a deep red, and he nodded.

I stepped forward and put my arms around him. "I'm so sorry you had to worry about that."

"I am going to marry Sarah someday, Mom."

"Okay. That doesn't surprise me and certainly won't surprise Auntie Karen. Sarah has announced it enough times, too," I chuckled.

He smiled. "Yes, she has."

"If you're alright then, I'll head out to see Grandmother."

"I'm not going to volunteer today. Grandfather left me enough money to do something on my own. I told them I needed a few days to work out some things. I'm setting up a spreadsheet to list some of the ways I might be able to help the Pueblo community financially. Will you review it with me after I get it done?"

"Yes, I'd be happy to sit with you. I have something you might want to consider. Tom Little Horse's ranch is going up for sale, and that might be a good investment for you while, at the same time, it can help some of those in need."

A smile spread across his face. "That would be so cool."

"We can talk about it later, okay?" I asked as I kissed him goodbye.

\*\*\*

When I got to Grandmother's house, Karen greeted me at the door, shaking her head, fighting tears. "It doesn't look good, Rosie. She's taken a turn for the worse. You'd better call Isabella."

My heart dropped, and I felt sick, knowing Karen was speaking the truth. Instead of going inside, I stepped back outside and called Isabella. "It's time, sweetheart …."

I called Mike to tell him what was happening and that I'd be with Grandmother. "Can you pick up Isabella at the airport and bring her here?"

"Of course, just do what you must, and don't worry, I'll take care of everything else, hear?"

"I'm so scared, Mike. I'm afraid I won't be able to let her go."

"My queen, you always do the right thing; that's who you are. I love you."

"I love you too, Mike."

"I'll see you when I bring Isabella. Meantime, call me if you need me, okay?"

"Thanks." "Please, God, give me the strength to do and say the right things," I whispered. I closed my eyes and took in a deep breath. I slowly walked to the door and let myself inside.

When Grandmother saw me walk into her bedroom, she brightened, but my heart dropped when I saw her. Although her eyes were bright, her face was gray, and her breathing had become shallow. She was serene and said,

"Do not be afraid. I'm not going anywhere yet, so take that worry off your face, my daughter."

I smiled and stepped forward to sit on the other side of Grandmother, opposite where Karen sat. I reached for Grandmother's hand and brought it to my lips. "I love you, Grandmother—my mother."

"And I, you, Little Bird," calling me my Indian name in a lifetime that I shared with her as her daughter.

"Have you been here long, Karen?" I asked.

She nodded.

"Why don't you go home and rest? I'll stay with Grandmother."

"Angel will be here after work. I'll bring over some dinner for everyone. Is there anything I can get you, Grandmother?" Karen asked.

"No, but thank you, dear sister," she answered through several puffs of air, referring to Karen as her sister in a previous lifetime.

Grandmother gently pulled her hand from mine. "Need to rest."

"Alright. I'm right here if you want anything. Isabella will be here soon, too."

Grandmother looked my way and nodded, grateful.

I stretched out on the bed beside Grandmother and held her close. Soon, she was asleep, making it hard for me to keep my eyes open. It wasn't long before we both were asleep.

# CHAPTER 35

I t was dark outside when I heard the noise at the front door and footsteps heading our way. Isabella rushed forward as Mike stood in the doorway, taking in the scene before him. Grandmother stirred, and as soon as she saw Isabella, she stretched out her hand to come closer.

Isabella knelt beside the bed and took Grandmother's hand, kissing it. "Oh, Grandmother, I'm so glad to see you."

Mike came forward and bent to kiss Grandmother on the cheek. "Hello, handsome," she whispered with a smile, knowing Mike was shy about her calling him that. "Hear my words on the wind and think of me with a smile," she puffed out between breaths.

Then Mike said something in Tewa to her. I didn't catch it all, but I heard the word for love in it. He raised her hand and kissed it. "Journey well, Grandmother."

Mike tipped his head for me to follow him out of the room. He held me close in the hallway and whispered, "I see it won't be long now, Rosie. Are you okay?"

I squeezed him tight and nodded. "Yes, I'll be fine. Is Jack here?"

"Yes, he wants to say goodbye to Grandmother too," he said, kissing me quickly before leaving the room.

Jack strode to Grandmother's side, looking like both his fathers with his dark looks and strong, physical body. I watched him closely as he bent down and said in a low voice, "Thank you for caring for my father when he needed you. Please say hello to him for me. Tell him I love him, and I'll do what I can for the Navajo Indians and all the others. Promise me?"

She blinked her eyes in acknowledgment.

"I love you, Grandmother. I hope your spirit will visit me often. Thank you for everything you have taught me."

Upon hearing his words, Grandmother's eyes teared.

Seeing that, Jack turned away, emotionally upset, and left the room.

Isabella noticed my emotions and patted the seat beside her on Grandmother's bed. I sat close to her, and as she had often done, she connected our hands with Grandmother's, making our three energies one. When she did, I felt light-headed, and it was as if I were being swept along a funnel going backward in time. Everything flew by fast enough that I couldn't make out any clear images until I stood on that pathway again with my little sister and mother collecting herbs in that lifetime we shared long ago. It was like watching a re-run show on television where I knew exactly what would be said and done. Helplessly, I watched and listened to my mother asking, "Little Bird, where is your sister? You're supposed to be watching her."

I looked on as I searched behind me and saw no one. "Little One, where are you?" I called out, terror in my heart. Then, my mother and I ran back down the path we had followed, calling out to my little sister. My heart was heavy with sorrow and shame that I had let my sister out of sight. When we rounded the bend where I knew my sister lay dead from a snake bite, my mother and I were surprised to see my sister smiling, holding out a bunch of flowers to us that she held in her hands.

My mother and I looked at each other in wonderment. What had happened? We knew that Little One had died in that lifetime, and now she was alive? Little One opened her mouth and spoke adult words in a deep voice, not hers. "Any karma or worries due to my death has been cleansed. In this lifetime you now share, you three have loved each other unconditionally, which alone has cleared all the negativity of the past. You are now released from the guilt and anguish you've carried all this time."

My mother stretched her arms to wrap my sister and me against her. As soon as she held us tight, I heard a whooshing noise, and I was back in real-time, sitting on Grandmother's bed with her and Isabella. Grandmother opened her eyes wide, and the three of us looked at each other in amazement. "Did you?" I asked.

Both Isabella and Grandmother squeezed my hands tighter, and Isabella nodded. Tears trailed our faces, and we could find no other words. Grandmother's eyes closed, and she smiled as her breaths became shorter. I rose and bent to kiss Grandmother's cheek. "I love you, Grandmother—my mother. Thank you for everything. I'll bring in the others."

Angel, Nica, Karen, Coyote, Sarah, Thomas, and Terrance came into the room and formed a circle around the bed. After each of them had kissed Grandmother's cheek and spoken a few private words, Karen and Coyote stepped to one side of the bed and held one of Grandmother's hands together. Angel and Nica went to the other side of the bed and held the other hand. Jack and Mike joined us, Jack standing next to Sarah, holding her hand while Mike came to my side. Then, the Pueblo Chieftain stepped into the room, and we all shed tears as we listened to him beat softly on his drum and begin his haunting chanting. It was surreal but oddly comforting to know her spirit would soon be free to roam the earth, according to his words.

When death comes calling, do we have the right to deny its duty? Are we wrong not to allow it to happen as it will? I selfishly fought to change what was happening before me, but I didn't know how I could. I stood next to Mike and Isabella at the foot of the bed, foolishly wishing Grandmother's life not to end. Then, just before we heard her final death rattle, I saw her spirit lift from her body, now motionless. Isabella grabbed my arm. "Mama, did you see that?"

"Yes, darling girl, it was beautiful, wasn't it?" I asked as I gathered her to me. Mike's arms wrapped around our shoulders, and we leaned into him, grateful for his love, kindness, and strength as we sobbed at our loss.

# CHAPTER 36

T he next few days became a blur for me. My heart ached at the loss of not having Grandmother in my life. I felt so alone—an odd sensation for someone surrounded by love from her family and friends. It was as if her death had taken some of my joy of living with her. I reviewed the losses I'd suffered and urged myself to look at them from a different perspective, for hadn't I been blessed to have had those people in my life in the first place? No matter how much I tried to see the bright side of things, I fought hard not to enter the dark place of depression.

Mike was well aware of my situation since he'd come to know me well throughout the years. Two weeks later, he came home with a surprise for me. He'd found a kennel that bred Silky Terrier puppies and handed me a little girl that I swear was Sweet Pea reincarnated. I immediately named her Ditto, much to the delight of Mike. It was a term I'd used to repeat his love for me back to him, and we used it between us now and then as a private message to recall that time.

Mike had done well with his choice of gifts. I had forgotten how much time and energy a puppy took, and it was only because Mike agreed to help that she remained with us. Ditto was too much for me to handle alone. Jack's dog, Miko, looked upon the puppy as little more than an irritant, but she graciously took on the trainer role and nipped at Ditto whenever she strayed out of line. The two dogs lifted our spirits, and we chuckled at all their antics.

It turned out that Mike was not interested in selling the Vegas office, and after much discussion, Brian returned to Boston. They'd agreed that when Brian no longer wanted the business, they would either sell it or Mike would buy him out. For the moment, Brian decided he was too young to retire. This pause gave them time to plan more for their later years. As long as the work in Vegas continued the way it was, Mike could take more time off and still receive his salary, as could Brian. And that seemed to satisfy both of them.

I decided to take some time to myself, and I left Ditto with Mike and headed down to the Chic Boutique for a change of scenery. I pulled into the back of the store. Since I didn't have my key with me, I knocked on the back door to let Angela know I was there and to let me in.

When Angela peeked through the cracked door, she looked frantic, and I watched her shake her head several times with tiny movements. "I don't have time for you today, Rosie. I'm busy. You'll have to come back another day."

Since this was so unlike Angela, it was clear that something was wrong. I nodded and said calmly, "I got your message, and I know I should have called. But no worries, I'll return later."

A brief sense of relief flashed across her face as she understood my message to her. She closed the door, and I heard Angela shake the lock after me. But it didn't click, and I knew she'd faked locking it. I immediately stepped away and grabbed my cell phone to call Coyote. "Angela is in trouble. Someone is inside the store. Hurry!"

"I'm on my way."

In a matter of minutes, I saw his car pass the alley where I stood and head to the front of the store without his siren blasting. I waited beside the back door and listened for signs that Coyote was inside. Soon I heard a commotion, and a shot rang out, followed by a scream. I leaned closer to the door, and as I did, the door burst open, knocking me to the ground. Before I knew what was happening, I was being hauled up with an arm around my neck, closing off my air. I raised both hands to pull his arm away from my throat, moving it enough for me to draw deep breaths. As soon as he spoke, I knew it was Harry. "Don't fight me, or I'll shoot you."

My heart pounded as he began to drag me along, my body protecting him as he made his way toward his car parked in the alley. He pushed me into the vehicle's passenger side, pointing his gun at me while scrambling into the driver's seat. As we began to pull out at top speed, Coyote emerged from the back door, aiming his gun at Harry and yelling for him to stop. That distracted Harry, and he inevitably pointed his gun back at Coyote. That gave me enough time to open my car door and roll out as he lurched forward, wheels spinning. "Fuck!" I heard him say as he picked up speed, leaving me behind.

I landed hard on my right side, with my hand blocking the fall. I heard a snapping sound and realized I must have broken a bone as pain shot through my arm. Coyote ran after Harry's car, continuing to yell for him to stop. When he reached me lying on the ground, he helped me onto my feet. Pressing his radio to his mouth, he gave orders to his officers, telling them where Harry was heading. "You'll be able to cut him off there. I'm on my way."

Coyote turned to me. "I've called the medics to come to check out Angela. I don't think she's injured; just scared. Have them look at your arm too. It looks like you broke it."

I entered the back of the store and found Angela sitting at the manager's desk, sobbing. She looked up with sadness. "Why do I have to keep paying for choosing the wrong boyfriend?"

When she noticed me grimacing, she rose from her seat. "What is it, Rosie? Are you hurt? Here, sit down," she said, tenderly guiding me into the chair she'd just vacated.

The medics pushed through the door, studying the two of us. "Which one of you is Angela?"

"I am, although you'd better look at Rosie's arm first. I think it's broken."

The medics wanted us to go to the hospital, but Angela refused. She needed to assure her salesladies that even though she'd been held hostage by Harry, all was okay, and they were safe. She was determined to keep the store open as if nothing had happened. I knew it was her way of dealing with the situation, and I couldn't blame her. Instead of going with the medics, I called Mike to come for me.

Mike was quiet as we drove to the hospital so they could set my arm. I glanced at him. "Don't say anything, okay?" It still bothered me that he and Brian thought trouble followed me everywhere I went. I had to admit that sometimes it seemed that way. Yet, things had slowed down as I'd grown older, and I was grateful for that.

By the time we reached home, the news was that Harry hadn't made one of the dangerous turns on the back roads during the car chase with the sheriff and police. Instead, he'd lost control of his car and had driven into a tree. It had killed him instantly and had happened exactly as Jack had predicted, which caused a backlash because others had heard what he'd told Harry.

For the rest of the summer, Jack was strangely ignored or taunted by some of Harry's friends, pointing at him and calling him names. I had to give Jack credit because it appeared that didn't bother him, but I knew better. He refused to allow any of their negativity to hinder him, yet others would always look at him differently now, and I knew he felt that. All the summer experiences had changed him from a boy to a man fully aware of his power and greater responsibilities.

# CHAPTER 37

**B**y the end of the summer, we all were anxious to return to Las Vegas—even Jack, who had become more attached to Sarah than ever before. They were like two peas in a pod, comfortable with each other like Isabella and Sammy had been at that age. But the truth was that it wasn't the same for any of us without Grandmother being with us in person. It was as if a cloud permanently hung over us, and we found it difficult to appreciate the sunshine.

With Cal no longer alive, Virginia didn't spend as much time in Santa Fe, making their absences even more noticeable. Isabella, Sammy, and the twins hadn't visited us in Santa Fe all summer, creating another void. I was having difficulty adjusting to the changes and was looking forward to being home in the warm desert weather.

Before we left, Jack made the final arrangements to become the new owner of Tom Little Horse's ranch. Luckily, he found that the husband/wife team, who had taken care of the property for the previous owners, wanted to continue their role. They would live in the small cottage constructed by the former owners on the property back by the barn. As part of the sales agreement, the ranch would continue to be a working farm with the animals remaining and the equipment to run the hay fields. A vegetable garden was mainly void now of produce except for a few squash and pumpkins.

When I visited the ranch with Jack and the realtor, I didn't think it would bother me as much as it did. The image of Tom lying on the ground with his life fading away kept flashing before me, opening a wound I thought had healed long ago. It had been so painful to lose him when I thought Mike was romantically involved with his employee back in Boston and it was Tom whom I would marry.

Seeing that the past owners had made a few improvements to the ranch was nice. They had added a master suite more extensive than Tom had, making it more private if guests were there. They had also expanded the corral to teach horseback riding and hold small horse shows. Jack had conceived the idea of turning the ranch into a place for wayward boys who would work the farm to make it self-sufficient. Both Isabella and I agreed that this idea would be something the Trust could support. I knew Cal would agree if he were alive.

Jack would be in his senior year at school and had earned enough credits to graduate at yearend instead of in June with the rest of his class. He had yet to decide whether to attend college the following fall or take a break from schooling for a year or two. He had discussed this idea with Mike and me, and we were open to him taking time away from studies if, and only if, he'd be doing something worthwhile.

As much as I couldn't wait to get back to Las Vegas, it was challenging to say goodbye to Karen, her crew, and Maria and her brood. They were my Western family, and I'd miss them. Luckily, I'd see Romano, Randy, Mimi, and Charles soon because I realized how much more their friendship meant to me after losing Grandmother.

That night, we had a massive barbeque at Maria's house, with Karen's family joining us. I was happy to see Maria and Karen had become like sisters. It was interesting to see how Maria's kids had become so grown up with Rosa, her youngest, nearing 20 years old, dating a very handsome chef—something that made me smile since food was something dear to Rosa's heart. Her boys were all involved in Miguel's landscaping business, which had expanded throughout the state and now included snowplowing. Maria and Miguel had reached a happy stage in life, and it was good to see how easily they laughed and enjoyed each other's company.

Karen was struggling as much as I was at losing Grandmother. Always protective of her, Coyote tenderly placed his arm around her, keeping her close for most of the night. Their boys were active teenagers and, like Sarah, very good-looking. They were heavily involved in sports at school and excelled in them, competing with each other as brothers do. Coyote was proud of them, but Sarah was his little princess, like many fathers with daughters.

I brought Ditto to the party with us, and she soon became the center of attention, with all of us laughing at her antics with Maria's dog. It was a beautiful night with the smell of autumn and the sounds of contentment being voiced. Grandmother would have loved being here with all of us. Knowing this, I searched for signs of her presence but found none. Before long, it was time to bid everyone goodbye until we returned for Thanksgiving.

Instead of Jack returning to the house with us, he was staying behind with Sarah. They had been in deep conversations the whole night, and I wondered what they were discussing. Sarah didn't look happy, but then again, neither did Jack.

\*\*\*

Sarah had offered to drive us to the airport, and we'd happily accepted her offer. When she arrived, we loaded our things into her SUV, and it felt like old times to have a dog carrier beside me. Ditto was inside, happy to be settled between Mike and me in the back seat. Mike reached for my hand and lifted it to his mouth, kissing our clutched hands. He smiled at me and winked, hoping to lift my spirits.

"Hey, handsome ..."

"I love you, Rosie."

"Ditto," I smiled.

At hearing her name, Ditto began to whine.

Realizing what'd happened, Mike and I chuckled.

"What's going on back there?" Jack asked playfully.

"Your mother is taunting the dog," teased Mike with a laugh.

"What can I say?" I answered, squeezing Mike's hand hard, causing him to yelp.

When we arrived at the airport, Sarah pulled to the curb to let us out, and I turned to thank Sarah, only to find her in tears. She was outside huddled with Jack, his back to me. I couldn't help but overhear them as I gathered Ditto's carryall, and Mike got the suitcases out of the trunk.

"I don't want you to leave, Jack," she whispered.

"I don't want to leave either, but …."

"No, you don't understand! I don't want us to be apart."

"Sarah, come on, we've talked about this. It's only for a few months, and then we'll be together."

"I just don't want anything to happen to you."

"Nothing is going to happen, I promise you," he replied, wiping her tears away.

Listening to their words caused goosebumps to cross my body. I shivered with unease. Why would Sarah be worried about something happening to Jack? What had I missed?

When I met Mike's eyes, he raised his eyebrows in question. Not knowing what was going on between Jack and Sarah, I shrugged. We pulled all the suitcases to the outside check-in and waited for Jack to catch up. As he came our way, I blew a kiss to Sarah, who was still outside the car looking longingly at Jack's retreating body. She didn't respond.

"Is everything okay, Jack?" I asked.

"Sarah has had difficulty with Grandmother's passing and is worried about losing another one she loves. I'm not the only one she fusses over. I'm surprised Auntie Karen didn't say something to you. On the sly, she asked me if I saw another death sometime soon, and I told her no."

As we were high in the sky, I thought about Karen asking Jack for psychic information, and I realized how far I'd drifted from my abilities by keeping myself busy with the more mundane aspect of living. And in doing so, it'd made me less aware of what was going on around me. Spirituality and ideas beyond time have everything to do with awareness. Yet, my not being so aware had made it possible for me to avoid the kind of trouble I had always gotten into when I'd first met Mike and Brian. A part of me was sad to leave those days behind.

But things were different now. I understood that it was up to me to let our lives move on with grace and allow my children to have the freedom to live their own lives. It was time for all the family to let go of grieving over Grandmother's death and let her spirit fly without our sadness holding her back. Our love for her will remain in our hearts forever.

# CHAPTER 38

## Present Time – Ten years Later

I awoke with a start. I sat up in bed, rubbing my eyes to clear all the images that had flown through my mind in one long night of dreaming and reviewing my life. I looked at Mike beside me, snoring as he slept undisturbed. I wondered what having a dreamless, restful night would be like. I groaned as I stretched and looked around me. We were meeting Jack for breakfast, and I wondered what he wanted to discuss with us. He was pretty independent now that he was 27 years old, living most of his time in Santa Fe.

Isabella was going to be 40 years old soon. Several years earlier, when I learned she was unexpectantly pregnant, my grandmother told me the baby girl would be highly gifted psychically. I wanted to support Isabella by teaching

211

her how to cope and thrive with her gift. The first day I held Joslin in my arms, I found purpose in life again after drifting along for the last ten years.

I kissed Mike and got up to take a shower and get dressed. Afterward, Mike stood in the bedroom doorway. "Are you ready?" he asked. "It's time to meet Jack. I told him we'd meet him at the café for breakfast."

"I'll be right there," I called out, wondering again what Jack was up to that he wanted to talk with us.

When I entered the living room, Mike smiled. "All set?"

I nodded and walked toward him. Not wanting to begin the day without it, Mike reached for me to give me my morning kiss, which had become our habit.

"My, you look handsome this morning! I'm one lucky lady," I said.

"Yes, you are," he said with sparkling eyes. "I hope you always feel that way."

"So far, so good," I replied, playfully swatting his arm.

He laughed. "C'mon, sweetheart, let's go meet our boy."

Seconds after we sat at the table, I saw Jack searching for us in the café doorway. When Jack spotted us, he strode forward confidently, and his muscular, trim figure exuded good health. He was uniquely handsome with chiseled features, nearly black eyes, and dark hair showing a bit of early grey. Like mine, his apricot skin was unusual and set his looks apart. As soon as Mike noticed Jack, he stood up to greet him. Although Jack was not quite as tall as Mike, it was only noticeable when they stood eye to eye. They had always been close, and even now, Jack went first to Mike to clasp him on the shoulder, greeting him before he came to me.

"Hi, Pop! How goes it? Hi, Mom, how are you?" he asked as he kissed my cheek.

"Good, sweetheart," I answered.

"Have a seat, Jack," urged Mike. "The waitress will be here any second."

As if on cue, the waitress came to our table asking, "Coffee, everyone?"

We nodded, and she began to pour the dark liquid into the mugs already on the table. The delicious aroma made me hungry.

"Mom and Dad, I've something to tell you. I'm considering asking Amanda to be my wife, and I wanted your approval."

I looked at Mike, who smiled. "She's a beautiful girl and smart."

"Mom?"

"What changed your mind, Jack?"

"It's about time, don't you think?" he asked, sorrow flashing across his face. "Amanda's been very patient with me. It's time to make that commitment before she changes her mind."

I studied him. "That's not the best way to start a marriage, Jack ... because she's been patient," I said gently. I reached for his hand. "What about Sarah? You've always loved her, and now that she's free, aren't you curious to see if there's something there for the two of you?"

"You've never liked Amanda, have you, Mom?" he asked with an edge to his tone.

"That's not true. There are many things about Amanda that I think are admirable. She's a wonderful, beautiful person and smart like Mike said. But there's something to say about yearning for a person you love, wanting her to become a part of you as a couple. I've not seen that for you in this relationship."

Jack's face drooped. "The truth is that Sarah won't even return my calls, Mom. So, getting back together with her is out."

"You mean you feel so strongly about loving her, and because of her non-response, that's it? Jack Williams! What has gotten into you? Fight for them if you love someone and want them in your life! Ask your father. That's what he did for me."

Mike's cheeks grew pink. "Your mother is right. If I hadn't pursued her, even though I'd done her wrong, I would have lost her. I can't imagine my life without her in it. She's brought me so much love and happiness along with you, Isabella, and the large family she and Isabella created. I want you to be as happy in your relationship as I've been with your mother."

Jack's eyes welled up. "Thanks, Dad."

"I think your mother's right. It's never too late. Fight for Sarah if she is the person you want in your life. If it's right, a second marriage for anyone can be significantly better than the first one."

"You were married before Mom? I didn't know that."

Mike and I looked at each other and smiled.

"There's a story, alright. Your Uncle Brian got me drunk in Las Vegas when we first became partners. Unknowingly, he and his friends got me hitched to one of the call girls as a joke."

"Uncle Brian. He's such a jokester." Jack laughed.

"It wasn't so funny when I found out," I added, still peeved at the memory.

"I'm sure," said Jack, trying to hold back a smile.

"Don't let Sarah's one unhappy marriage hold you back from getting what you want, Jack," continued Mike. "This is an opportunity to correct what went wrong between you and Sarah."

Jack shook his head. "She blames me for her getting married—said I should have stood up and not allowed her to marry her husband. And not doing so makes it my fault?" Miserable, he looked to Mike for the answer. "What did she expect me to do? She'd already agreed to marry the jerk. Where did that leave me?"

Mike and I were silent.

"Dammit, you're right, Mom and Dad." Jack sighed. "Okay, I'll do better than call her. I'll fly to Santa Fe to talk to her face-to-face. Please, Mom, don't say anything to Auntie Karen. I know how close you two are, but I want to surprise Sarah without anyone knowing I'm coming, okay?"

"Fair enough," I said.

Mike patted Jack's arm. "It's not easy to understand women. Just remember that all you have to do is love them and agree with them," Jack admitted reluctantly.

"Now hold on, you two," I protested, laughing.

"Seriously, Jack. Always tell your lady love that you love her. Things will usually work out then," urged Mike.

"As long as you're sincere about loving her," I added.

Mike squeezed my hand. "Yes, my queen, you're right," he agreed, winking at Jack.

We left the restaurant after a leisurely buffet. Jack's spirits seemed lighter. He and Mike had a golf tee time for that afternoon. I was happy to be dropped off at home since I could see a wedding in my immediate future.

# CHAPTER 39

T hese days I had more time on my hands and had become bored with life. So, several days after we'd met Jack for breakfast, I jumped at the chance when Roberto called to ask me to help him on a case. Looking back, I found it hard to dismiss the thrill of assisting Mike and the Chief of Police in finding a lost one or helping solve a murder.

Excitement filled me as I entered the police station; I had a renewed sense of purpose. Roberto was convinced that if Isabella and I worked together as we had before, we could help him out.

I was immediately ushered into Roberto's office, where Isabella was already seated. I greeted her with a kiss and then shook Roberto's hand. "It's nice to see you again, Rosie. I'm hoping that the two of you will be able to help me with this case. It's getting nowhere," he said, "and if we don't solve it soon, it won't get the attention it deserves."

"What do you have so far?" I asked.

Roberto pulled photos from the file folder before him and handed them to me for Isabella and me to see. What I saw sickened me. A small woman was lying on the ground, arms and legs misaligned, looking as if she had been tossed aside like a ragdoll who had seen better days. She was an older lady, probably in her 70s, with beautiful white hair pulled to the top of her head in a knot. Oddly enough, her dark face was relatively youthful, and she looked resigned to her fate despite blood pooling around her head.

"How sad," Isabella said. "How did she die?"

"Blunt force to the head," Roberto answered.

"Are you wanting us to figure out who killed her?" I asked, confused.

Robert looked surprised. "Oh, I thought I'd told you why I needed your help. It's this woman's granddaughter who has gone missing! We're looking for her to see if she knows why anyone would want to kill her grandmother. If we find her, maybe she can lead us to the murderer. We also want to make sure she's safe."

Isabella and I looked at each other in disbelief. "She's missing?" Isabella asked.

Roberto nodded. "She's 16 years old, looks more like 26, I might add. She's gone missing ever since her grandmother was killed. When my deputy went to the house to let them know what'd happened, he discovered her granddaughter lived with her. He told the granddaughter he needed to call Child Services and for her to pack a bag. He waited for her and went to find her when she didn't show up. She had taken off—crawled out her bedroom window. We haven't been able to find her. She could be "surfing" couches at her friends' houses or hiding on the streets. But what worries us is that no one has seen or heard from her since. However, I believe she's still here in Vegas."

"What do you have on her?" I asked.

"Here, let me show you her picture and other information we've gathered. We tried to track down the girl's mother but haven't found anything, which is probably why she was living with her grandmother."

"I'd like a copy of her photo and anything to do with the girl," Isabella said.

"Me, too," I added.

Roberto nodded and called for the desk clerk. "Can you please make two copies of this?"

The clerk entered the room and smiled when she saw Isabella sitting there. "Hi there, Isabella. Long time no see."

"Hi, Margaret, how are you?" Isabella asked, smiling.

"I'm good." She grimaced at seeing the information to be copied. "It's getting old seeing so many young girls gone missing. Good luck with this one; I hope you find her."

"Mike and Sammy aren't involved in this case?" I asked Roberto.

"No, not yet. You two might have a better chance of finding the girl because you are women. Our guys have had some difficulty getting anything out of her friends. Sometimes men have a harder time; you know how it is."

"Fair enough," I said.

I jumped in surprise when I heard, "Hi, Gramma Rose!"

At twelve years old, Joslin had her father's looks with light blond wavy hair and large blue eyes the color of a cloudless summer day. She had Isabella's slim build, and she wore an inquisitive expression. Her advanced psychic abilities made her curious to understand why people chose to do what they did until she learned that they had no extra prompting from outside sources as she did.

"Hi, sweetheart! What are you doing here?" I asked, holding my arms out to wrap around her.

"It's Take Your Child to Work Day!" Joslin said. "Since this is for school, Mom and Dad said I could come today."

"Oh," I responded, looking at Isabella with a raised brow.

"Sammy is out of town working for a client. So, she's with me," Isabella said with a wink.

"I understand," I said, gathering Joslin tighter and kissing the top of her head.

Handing us the copied pages in separate folders, Roberto asked, "Do you have all you want? Don't forget, if there's anything else you ladies need, call me."

After saying goodbye to Roberto, I turned to the girls. "I think it's about time for lunch. Shall we?"

Joslin and Isabella said in unison, "Yes."

"Where to, Gramma Rose?" Joslin asked as she tugged on my arm.

"How about we head to old town Las Vegas for Mexican food?"

"Yum," said Joslin, a fan of tamales.

\*\*\*

As we sat inside the restaurant and looked out, it was clear that our area was not the best because it was easy to see a few "ladies of the evening" already out, looking for their next customer. Joslin was studying them.

"Do those girls think that anyone is going to stop and pick them up with the two cops standing by?" asked Joslin.

"What do you mean?" I asked.

"See those two men over there pretending they're not interested in those girls. They're cops."

"How do you know that?" Isabella asked.

"Watch," she urged.

Sure enough, as a car pulled up beside the lady closest to us, the two men stepped forward and surrounded the vehicle, demanding the man step outside his car. One opened the car door to pull the driver out if he refused, while the other blocked the car from moving forward.

Both Isabella and I stared at Joslin in surprise. She looked between us and shrugged her shoulders as if knowing what would happen was nothing.

I was quiet while we ate, thinking about Joslin's psychic gift. Isabella and Sammy would have their hands full, guiding Joslin about the best ways to use her abilities as she made her way to adulthood. Maybe she'd follow in her parent's footsteps and work with the law to find lost children and murderers. I believed that for those with additional advantages, it was important not to view them as burdens.

After Joslin excused herself to go to the bathroom, Isabella interrupted my thoughts. "Mama, what do you think about showing Joslin the photo of the missing girl? Maybe she can help us. With her sensitivity, I feel she already knows what we're up to whether we tell her or not."

"I think it's important for us to be the ones to work with her as she begins to hone her talent, don't you agree?"

"Yes, I do. Let's go back home and sit down with Joslin together."

"Okay, I'll grab the bill and meet you at my house," I said.

221

THE WORLD.

# CHAPTER 40

A s soon as we settled around the table, Isabella told Joslin, "Gramma Rose and I are working on a case to find a missing girl. Your father and I hoped to hold off on including you in cases until you were older, but it seems your psychic ability has made it impossible to wait."

"Mama, I've always known I'd follow in your and Daddy's footsteps. Gramma Rose's and Uncle Jack's, too."

"You do not need to see any photos of the girl's grandmother who died. Just know that when the girl found out the police were going to put her into Child Services, she took off. Roberto and the others haven't been able to find her."

"What's her name, Mama?" Joslin asked.

"Sherah Jones. Here's her photo," Isabella said as she pushed the photo toward her.

"She's very beautiful," Joslin said. Then, she closed her eyes and sat still for a moment. "She's had a very sad life so far. Here, Gramma Rose, do you agree?"

Only when my hand touched Joslin's arm as she passed me the photo did a vision of a little girl come to me. I'd been away from using my psychic abilities too long to "see" Sherah's past alone. It proved to me that I needed to meditate more.

We spent time going over Roberto's notes using the computer to see what, if anything, we could find on social media about Sherah. She had a Facebook account that had been recently opened – about the same time she'd moved in with her grandmother, I'd guess. She did, indeed, look older than her 16 years with fake eyelashes and heavy makeup. Despite that, a tenderness about her expression made her look youthful – caught in that awkward in-between stage of child and adult. There was a sadness in her large hazel eyes that was hard to ignore, making me determined to find her and protect her.

We listed all the usual things – the name of the school, teachers, and classmates that Roberto had interviewed. We'd do our own interviewing. There was no notation of whether she had a cell phone or not. We'd need to check that out. She had to have one – all the kids did. I was getting the gist of what Roberto meant about his men being unable to get much information from her friends—there wasn't much. Her friends were protecting Sherah, not realizing they could do more harm than good. We also needed to find as much information as possible about Sherah's grandmother.

Neither Isabella nor I wanted Joslin tangled up in the murder; we were limiting her involvement to finding

Sherah. We both believed it was important for Joslin to be a "regular kid" for as long as possible.

While Joslin was in school the next day, Isabella and I would begin our interviews at Sherah's high school. I was interested to see what her homeroom teacher was like because, for some reason, I had an unsettling feeling about her. I'd have to push that aside since my pre-judging her could throw the investigation off.

We stopped what we were doing, and noticing the time, I asked, "It's too bad your boys aren't attending Sherah's high school. Do they have soccer practice this afternoon?"

She looked at her watch and said, "Yes, I'm supposed to pick them up at the field. Come on, Joslin."

"Can I stay with Gramma Rose? Please!"

I nodded that it was okay by me.

"Okay, then. Just be home by 8 o'clock," Isabella said. She kissed Joslin goodbye and turned to me. "This seems like old times. You and me working together?"

"Yes, sweetheart, it sure does. I hope we're lucky and we find Sherah right away. Kiss the boys for me, Isabella. I'll see that Joslin gets home later."

I watched Isabella leave and was filled with pride as I did every time I saw her. Joslin tugged on my arm. "Let's see if Papa Mike will grill us some steaks."

"Without a doubt, I bet you can talk him into that." Yup, she was a Foodie, just like Jack.

# CHAPTER 41

I picked up Isabella the following day and drove to the high school. As we sat in the office, waiting to speak to the principal and the homeroom teacher, I was amazed at how busy the place was with kids popping in for numerous reasons—tardy slips, health reasons, appointments with the school psychologist, and more. The soccer coach came in with a teenage boy to have him released from suspension now that he had a passing grade on his latest quiz. The coach recognized Isabella when he saw her. "Hi, Mrs. Brooks."

"Hi, it looks like Timmy will return to the team then, Coach? Congratulations!"

The coach winked at Isabella and held his thumb up in victory.

After they left, Isabella turned to me. "Remember Coach Johnson? He holds a summer soccer camp where the boys attend. He teaches history, too. He's always pushing kids to do well in school and works extra time with them to help them pass his class."

A scattering of goosebumps crossed my body. "Maybe he could help us by checking with the players to see if they know anything about Sherah."

Isabella said, "I was thinking the same thing. After all, with Sherah being so pretty, I bet one of the guys may know something."

A stern older woman marched past them and leaned against the doorframe of the principal's office. "You wanted to see me?" she asked in a bad-tempered tone.

"Yes, come on inside. I'll get the two ladies to join us." He peeked outside his door and waved us in.

Isabella and I took the two empty chairs before the principal's desk. Then, he introduced us. "Ms. Greenly, this is Mrs. Brooks and Mrs. Williams, here to see us about Sherah. The Chief of Police sent them."

Ms. Greenly jerked her head around to eye us with suspicion. I immediately thought the woman had no tolerance for anything outside her comfort zone—inflexible to change. She said, "What is it you want?"

Isabella took the lead. "We understand that Sherah was in your homeroom. What can you tell us about her?"

"She's trouble. She and her friends are more interested in attracting the boys than making something of themselves. Wearing makeup and clothes so short it's a sin. They just don't get it. Then they wonder why they get into trouble," Ms. Greenly ended in disgust.

"You do know, don't you, that Sherah's been missing for several weeks? Missing after her grandmother was murdered?" I asked.

"Yes, and I'm sorry about that. But really, there's nothing I can do about it," Ms. Greenly said with little empathy.

Sensing my displeasure with the teacher, Isabella jumped in. "We need you to list the names of Sherah's girlfriends and any boys she might have been involved with."

Principal Monahan stepped forward and handed Ms. Greenly a pen and paper. She began to write down names for us hurriedly.

"Was she a good student?" I asked.

Ms. Greenly paused and studied me. "She was smart—just didn't apply herself that much."

"She probably had a lot on her mind," I stated sarcastically. "Did you ever find her dozing off in your room before her classes?" I added.

She shook her head. "No, I didn't. She was usually busy on her phone. You know how kids are today—can't do anything without their cell phones. It's a shame they were even invented. Kids don't know how to write and spell anymore."

"Ahh, so she does have a cell phone then. Do either of you have her number?" asked Isabella, looking at the principal and Ms. Greenly. Both shook their heads.

"Did either of you ever meet Sherah's grandmother?" I asked.

Again, Ms. Greenly shook her head. Then, she handed me the list of names she'd written down as she rose from her chair. "If that's all, I need to get back to my room."

"Thank you for your time," Isabella said. "We appreciate it. If you think of anything, please give us a call."

I handed her a card with Isabella's and my cell phone numbers on the back and then did the same for the principal. "One question before you go, Ms. Greenly. What do you think could have happened to Sherah?"

Ms. Greenly stammered, "I have no idea. Why do you ask?"

"Wasn't there another girl who went missing a few years back? What happened to her?"

"We try not to talk about that incident because it's a cloud over the school." She looked to the principal. He nodded, indicating that he'd answer the question, and then he waved Ms. Greenly back to her class.

"Wasn't she murdered?" I urged.

The principal paused. "To answer your question, yes. Her body was found in the desert a few days later, and the killer was never found."

"How sad," Isabella said.

Goosebumps crossed my body, and I knew he was hiding something from us. "I can understand why you don't like talking about it, but is there something else you're not sharing about the case?"

The principal's face flushed, and he took a deep breath. "I told the police everything I know."

"When was the last time you saw her?" I pushed.

We waited, letting the silence demand to be filled. Finally, the principal spoke, "She came to me to discuss a problem, but I told her she'd have to see me later since I had another appointment. That was the day before she went missing, and I never saw her again."

"Did you tell the police that?" I asked.

"Of course, I did," he sputtered, "but nothing came of it." His phone rang, and with visible relief, he answered it. "Yes, please hold," he told the caller. He covered the phone's mouthpiece with his hand and looked at us. "I have to take this call. Is there anything else? If so, you know where to find me."

With that, we left and walked to our parked car to head home. We'd have to wait until the end of the school day to interview any of Sherah's friends.

At home, we began to break down the list of Sherah's friends. It was interesting to see that most of the people listed on Ms. Greenly's paper matched the list from Roberto's file. Luckily, Roberto's people had the address attached to the name and phone numbers for most. One name stood out for me—Evie Lynn—the first name on Ms. Greenly's list. Probably Sherah's best friend. A part-time job at Joe's Pizza was written next to her name.

"It looks like we're going to have to go for some pizza," I said.

"Why is that?" asked Isabella, curious.

"See here. Evie Lynn works part-time at Joe's Pizza," I said as I pushed my paper toward her.

Isabella smiled. "Lucky girl. His pizza is great!"

I chuckled. "Pizza was your favorite food when you were young."

"Still is," laughed Isabella patting my hand. "Let's go there for lunch and see what we can learn about Evie Lynn. That way, maybe we can figure out how to approach her about Sherah."

"That's fine by me," I agreed as I grabbed my purse and headed out.

# CHAPTER 42

**W**e arrived at Joe's Pizza after the rush lunch hour and had no trouble finding an empty booth. I saw two waitresses clearing tables, pocketing their tips. The older one lifted her hand and waved at us. "I'll grab some menus and be right with ya," she called to us.

When she returned, I lost myself in the menu, leaving Isabella to ask the waitress some questions.

"Does Evie Lynn still work here?" Isabella asked.

"Sure does," said the waitress. "She should be here later. Why?"

"I wanted to speak with her about her friend who's gone missing."

"You mean Sherah Jones?"

"Yes, that's the one."

"Evie Lynn gets mighty upset if anyone asks her questions like them police did. She don't like to talk about Sherah … says she don't know nothing about her gone missing. But I'm telling you," she leaned closer and whispered, "that sure as shootin' ain't true. They were like two peas in a pod. Evie Lynn's got to know something. Don't tell her I said anything, though."

"Whatever you say is between us," assured Isabella.

"Gloria! Stop your yakking and get their orders in before my break."

"Okay, boss! What do you ladies want?" she asked, all business now.

I ordered a large pepperoni pizza for us to eat. We took our time munching the pizza and making more notes. I'd take any leftovers home to Mike for a snack.

"I want to go back to the high school. The principal never answered whether he'd ever met Sherah's grandmother, and that's bothering me. Also, we don't know what classes Sherah was taking. What do you have, Isabella?"

"I want to check with my boys to see if they've heard anything. I doubt anyone from their private school knows anything, but you never know. Sometimes, they meet up with some of the kids from the local high school to play soccer for fun. I also think we should talk to Coach Johnson."

"Agreed. Are you free tomorrow, Isabella?"

"I'm not. I am meeting with the accountant to review some things for the Trust. But I'm free the following day."

"That's okay. I think I'll look into the grandmother's file folder and see if I can come up with something there. Her murder and Sherah being missing have to be tied together. It has to be more than the Child Services issue to make her flee, don't you think?"

"Yeah, I do. I'm just worried that the longer Sherah goes missing, the news won't be good."

The door swung open, and in walked Evie Lynn. She headed right to the back, but before she reached it, the older waitress said something to her, and Evie Lynn looked at us with a sad expression. Then, she immediately turned and raced out the door before either Isabella or I could react.

"Well, I guess speaking to Evie Lynn is now a lost cause," I said. "She wouldn't react that way if she knew nothing about Sherah's whereabouts. The waitress was right about that."

"We'll surprise her here one night soon and catch her after work," said Isabella.

"Sounds good. Do we have time to meet up with another of Sherah's friends before the kids get home from school?" I asked.

Isabella looked at her watch. "Why not? Maria's house is nearby, and her name lists no job."

Maria was the second friend written down on Ms. Greenly's list. We left a hefty tip and waved goodbye to the older waitress.

\*\*\*

We pulled up to a small house with a dirt lawn in North Las Vegas. We were surprised to find small children's toys scattered across the front yard and two empty Big-Wheel bikes pulled close to the porch. The mother heard us because she stood protectively inside the screen door with her arms crossed against her chest. She wore no smile, and apprehension showed on her face as we came closer.

"Whatcha want?" she hollered out.

"Is Maria here?" Isabella asked.

"Who wants to know?"

"We're here to talk to her about her friend, Sherah Jones."

"Well, Maria ain't here."

I stepped forward, "We're worried about Sherah. We want to find her before anything bad can happen to her."

"Are you with Child Services?" she asked as she stepped outside. "Cause if you are …."

"Not us," Isabella quickly injected. "We're private investigators trying to find Sherah and keep her safe. Too many things can happen to young girls left to their own devices."

"You got that right," the woman agreed. "Look, leave me your number, and I'll let Maria know you came by. I can't promise anything more than that. You know how teenage girls can be—can't make them do nothing they don't want to."

"Do you know Sherah?" I asked.

"You best talk to Maria," she answered.

I handed her our card with our names and telephone numbers. "Okay, thanks so much."

Without a word, she cracked open the door, grabbed the card, and turned away, letting the screen door slam behind her. We walked back to the car in silence.

# CHAPTER 43

I woke up to the smell of freshly brewed coffee. I climbed out of bed and padded my way down to the kitchen. As I stepped in, Mike greeted me with his morning kiss and a mug of java fixed precisely how I liked it.

"You're up early! What's going on?" I asked, stooping to pet Ditto.

"Sammy and I have a job to do up north. We should be back later tonight."

At my surprised look, he added. "There's nothing to worry about … just meeting a prospective client. Someone in his company has been stealing his products and mixing up the orders."

"That's sure frustrating for the owner," I commented.

"Exactly. What are you up to today, sweetheart?"

"I'm going to see Roberto about a murder that happened a month ago. Since then, the victim's granddaughter who'd been living with her has disappeared."

"I'm amazed that Roberto has you looking into the murder …."

"He hired Isabella and me to find the missing girl," I corrected.

"Well, if anyone can find her, you and Isabella can," he announced as he came closer and pinched my cheek affectionately. "Just be careful …."

"Don't say it, Mike."

"I know; I won't. I love you, my beautiful queen."

"Love you too, handsome."

\*\*\*

As soon as he walked out the door, the phone rang. I was pleased to see that it was my sister-friend, Karen. I'd promised Jack I wouldn't call Karen and wait to hear from her. Since Jack had left to surprise Sarah in Santa Fe a few days before, I'd kept my promise to him, but it had not been easy. Since Karen's daughter and Jack had been children, they had assumed they would marry, as did Karen and I. After a short, unhappy marriage for Sarah, she'd told Karen, "I'm through with men, period."

When Sarah accepted the proposal from a nice enough man, we all knew it wouldn't work. As much as we all talked to her about it, she refused to back down. After his last argument with Sarah before the wedding, Jack returned home and said, "Don't start, Mom. She's not going to listen to any of us. Especially now that she looks at it as a challenge."

"But …"

"Mom, you can't make someone love you just because you love them."

Now that she was free, he had a chance to win back her love. However, I knew Jack well enough to know that he wouldn't wait forever, especially since he was considering marrying Amanda, thinking he would be doing right by her. I was on pins and needles to discover what was happening in Santa Fe.

"Hey, Karen, how's it going?"

"Oh my! It's been quite a time. Jack certainly surprised all of us when he walked through the door yesterday. This morning, Jack talked Sarah into spending the weekend with him at his ranch. Since Jack arrived, she only agreed to go with him to escape me and my smiling face. I think Coyote would agree with that, too," she laughed.

I laughed with her. "So, was Sarah happy to see him?"

"She wanted nothing to do with him at first. I don't know what you and Mike said to that boy, but he's determined to claim Sarah as his true love. She finally relented and let him take her out to dinner last night. What the next few days bring about is anyone's guess."

"I hope that Sarah opens up her heart to Jack. He says he's tired of being alone and was thinking of marrying Amanda because he wanted to do right by her since they'd dated for so long. Amanda is lovely, but I don't see that working out for them in the long run. We both know that Jack and Sarah are meant to be together. They are two very stubborn people, though. Let's hope things work out between them."

"I have my bets on us becoming mothers-in-law. And I know it'd be just as good as your being mothers-in-law with Sammy's mother, Maggie. Wouldn't that be a hoot?"

"Yes, we'd have much fun with that," I laughed.

Karen's home phone rang, and she said, "Sorry, but I have to run. Don't worry. I'll keep you in the loop and let you know immediately if anything new happens."

"That's a deal," I said. "Love you."

"Love you, too. Bye."

I looked at my watch and decided to get dressed and head over to see Roberto about the murder of Sherah's grandmother. I had the horrible feeling that she'd been killed simply because she was Sherah's grandmother, and I wondered who would have a reason to kill a pretty older woman.

# CHAPTER 44

**W**hen I got to the police station, I had to wait to see Roberto. He was busy with another person shouting at him in a loud voice extending beyond the enclosed office. Since I'd first met Roberto years ago, his dark hair had turned primarily grey, and it was easy to see why that'd happened. His job was difficult, especially in Las Vegas, where there were many murders and people went missing. I marveled at his calm demeanor as he let the man spill his venom. Then, in a lower tone, he said something I couldn't hear to the man, and all the air of anger became deflated as the man sat down and held his head in his hands. Roberto then patted the man on the shoulder and guided him out of the office.

When Roberto saw me, he smiled. "C'mon in, Rosie, and take a seat. I'll be right back."

I sighed, impatient for Roberto to return. I sat in one of the two chairs positioned in front of his desk piled with different folders, making it evident that unlawfulness in Las Vegas was booming. It was crushing to realize that humans always try to stretch the boundaries of what's morally right, much less legally correct. I wondered if our society today was making it easier and easier to step outside that line.

Roberto came into the room with a smile. "This is a pleasant surprise. I wasn't expecting you this morning. What can I do for you, Rosie?"

"I'd like to see the folder on Sherah's grandmother. I'm certain her murder ties to Sherah, but I don't know how it's connected yet. I'm hoping that by studying her murder, something comes to me."

"Sure." He picked up the phone. "Margaret, can you bring in the file on Mrs. Jones and see if Roger is here? If so, tell him to join us. Thank you." He turned to me. "I've asked for Roger to join us since he was the first one on the scene of the murder. Maybe he can add something."

Margaret handed Roberto the folder and said, "Hi there, Rosie. No Isabella today?"

I smiled at Margaret. "No, she couldn't make it this morning, but I'll tell her you asked for her."

"Anything else, Chief?" Margaret asked.

"No, thank you. That's all," he replied, handing me the file.

When I touched it, a vision came to me of Mrs. Jones arguing with someone. I searched through the file until I found the autopsy report. After I read it, I asked, "So she died from a blow to the head?"

"Yes, that's right."

"Could that be caused by her being pushed, falling, and hitting her head?"

"That's possible," said the Chief, lost in thought.

Roger came through the door. "You wanted me, Chief?"

"C'mon in. You know Rosie, don't you?"

"Sure do. How are you, Rosie?"

I smiled. Roger was an older officer on the force for many years. He was a good man—one I respected. "The Chief says that you are the one who found Mrs. Jones ...."

"That's right. Poor lady."

"Did she have her purse with her?"

"Yes, but no money was taken."

I sat in silence for a moment. "What did the medical examiner have to say?"

"He said she'd died from a blow to the back of the head," Roger answered.

"That's what I thought." The Chief and Roger looked at me, waiting for me to clue them into my thinking. "I think she was arguing with someone, and when they pushed her, they didn't expect her to fall and die."

"That could be," Roberto said, looking at the autopsy report with a puzzled expression. "Now we need to find out who that someone might be."

"With your permission, I'd like to speak to the Medical Examiner."

"Sure, Rosie, go ahead. Let me know if you come up with anything."

I rose from my chair and handed the file folder back to Roberto.

"Keep in touch and stay safe, or Mike will have my head!" he warned.

I tossed my head in annoyance. I was never going to live down some of my previous adventures. I forced a smile. "I might say the same thing to you, Chief. Stay safe, and thanks for your time. Goodbye, you two."

My mind was going in different directions as I left the station. I hopped into the car and drove the short distance to the morgue, where I would talk to the Medical Examiner.

I'd concluded that to be a Medical Examiner, one had to be different from the average person to take on that role. I'd dealt with three different ones so far—all odder than their predecessor. Harry Steemer (the newest one) took the cake. He was strange-looking with a prominent forehead, tiny eyes, and a sense of humor that was darker than midnight. Yet, doing what he did, I understood that was his way of dealing with the aftermath of what horrible things were done to others.

As I entered the morgue, delicious smells drifted out to me. Despite dealing with dead bodies all the time, Harry was a Foodie and let nothing get in the way of enjoying his meals. He had a separate kitchen area with an inside grill, which he often used. Despite myself, my stomach growled, anticipating what he might be cooking. I'd never let myself give in to the temptation of sharing a meal with him there, and I vowed that today wouldn't be an exception.

"Well, well, look what the Universe brought me today!" Harry exclaimed when he saw me. "Rosie, pull up a chair and join me."

"Not today, Harry. Another day, maybe."

"You always say that. What can I do for you?"

"Mrs. Jones, the old lady murdered a month ago."

"Ah, the one with a blow to the back of her head. Yes?"

"Did she have any bruise marks on her upper body?"

"Why do you ask?"

"I believe she argued with someone and was pushed. I don't think the murderer killed her intentionally."

He closed his eyes for a few moments. I'd heard that he had a photographic memory, and I shivered at the thought that he'd always be able to pull horrid memories to the forefront. "Hmm. I think you can go to the head of the class, missy. She had a broken collar bone and bruises around it."

"How come that wasn't listed on the autopsy report, Harry?"

"Probably because that fool intern wrote up the report. I had to fire him after three days on the job," he said disgustingly. "Are you looking for part-time work, Rosie? I have an opening for an assistant."

"No, Harry, but thanks for the offer."

"If you change your mind for any reason, let me know, okay?" He hesitated, "Liver and onions are on the menu today. Are you sure you won't join me?"

"No, no. I have to run. I'll let you get back to your meal, and thanks so much for your help." I didn't think I'd ever be able to look at liver and onions the same way again.

As I drove away, I felt confident I'd put one piece of the puzzle in place.

# CHAPTER 45

I telephoned the school principal at Sherah's high school and asked for a copy of the classes that Sherah was taking. He told me he'd have the guidance counselor copy her schedule and have it waiting in the office for me to pick up later in the day.

I called Mimi to see if, by chance, she was available for lunch. We decided to meet at Rosalie's, where she sometimes worked as a hostess, a task she liked to do to keep an eye on the place. She was still a silent partner in the business, along with her husband, Charles. Romano and Randy remained the majority owners, something that Romano and Mimi had set up from the start of their partnership.

No matter how much time passed, I was always thrilled to see my name on one of the most famous restaurants in the valley. Thanks to Mimi's input, it was still a beautifully designed place with outstanding landscaping. Gardening was not my forte.

I chose a corner seat in one of the smaller eating areas to wait for Mimi. I was pleased to see my dear friend cross the room confidently to meet me. The years had been kind to her, and she was more beautiful and younger-looking than the first day I'd seen her. A loving relationship with a man she adored and who adored her had served them well. And I was glad for her.

"Hi, darling girl," Mimi said.

"Hi, yourself, my dear friend," I responded.

"Golly, I have missed you, Rosie!"

"What's it been … two weeks since we've seen each other?" I laughed.

Mimi chuckled. "What's going on, Rosie?"

"I'm working with Isabella on a new case of a missing girl. And I must tell you, it feels good to be back," I smiled.

"You've missed it?"

"If I'm honest, Mimi, no one needs me anymore. The kids are off on their own—Isabella with her own family. And possibly Jack with a new family of his own soon. It's not that I'm in the way or they want to spend all their time without Mike and me. It's just that they have their own lives to live, and I need to allow them that space."

Mimi patted my hand. "I know what you're saying. Charles' family is the same, and we've decided to let them do their own thing *most* of the time. However, Charles put his foot down on wanting us all to get together for Christmas. So far, it's been working."

The waitress came by, setting two glasses of chilled sauvignon blanc before us. "Compliments of the chef." The waitress was young with a pleasant face. "Chef Romano asked if you wanted him to surprise you with a meal for two."

Pleasure lit up our faces, and we both nodded. "That would be lovely," I confirmed.

The waitress smiled. "Good."

After she left, I turned to Mimi, "How are you feeling?"

"Good. A bit sad, though, to see some of my female plumbing go. Not that it ever did me any good," Mimi chuckled.

"I remember you telling me that having children was never in the cards for you. Are you unhappy about that?" I asked tenderly.

"No, not really. Besides, Charles' children and grandchildren are now mine too. And they're great kids. So, I'm lucky."

"How could they not love you, Mimi?" I asked, patting her hand this time.

"Here you go, ladies," the waitress interrupted.

"Careful, the plates are hot," reminded the server as he placed them in front of us.

I loved good food, especially the way Romano cooked it. I was excited to see a beautiful plate of Sole Meuniere, one of my favorite French dishes. Romano had added lemon and capers to the brown butter covering the fresh-looking sole, making it look almost too good to eat. That thought didn't last long as I eagerly dug in. After the first bite, I swooned with pleasure.

We were nearly finished when Romano approached our table wearing a smile. My eyes lit up when I saw him. I loved him dearly. He bent and kissed us on both cheeks as the French do.

"You outdid yourself with the Sole Meuniere, Romano. It was so fresh and light. Perfecto!"

As any good chef does, Romano basked in his compliment. "Ah, Rosebud, you know just what to say to win a man's heart," he laughed.

"A handsome, overweight chef's heart, I might add," chuckled his partner, Randy, leaning in to kiss me. "How are you, darlin'?"

"I'm fine, my friend. When are you and Romano leaving for Paris?"

"Not for a few weeks yet. Want to join us?"

Returning to Paris was tempting, but the timing wasn't right. "Not this time, but let me know the next time you two plan to go back, and I'll try to make that happen."

"Fair enough," he said.

They left us, stopping at various other tables to greet customers. I watched them, proud to be their friend. I turned to Mimi, "So you and Charles will take over the restaurant while they're gone?"

"Yes, we haven't done that for a while, so both of us might be out of practice, but we'll be fine. The new sous chef is great, and she'll be a big help."

"Call me if you need a hostess for a night or two."

"Good to know," Mimi smiled.

We walked out of the restaurant together, parting with the promise of touching base at the end of the week. Charles and Mike often played golf together when they could, and I thought I'd overheard Mike on the phone with Charles talking about a golf game this upcoming weekend.

As I drove away from the restaurant, I warmed at the thought that I was blessed to have so many beautiful friends. I headed for the high school to pick up Sherah's class schedule. I'd be curious to see what she was taking. Isabella and I were meeting in the morning to review everything again. As I was pulling into the schoolyard, my phone rang. I pulled the phone from my pocket, and when I answered it, I heard silence before everything went dead.

\*\*\*

I pushed my way inside the school as it released students, anxious to leave at the end of the day. I went to the office and was again amazed at how busy it was. After several students were directed to a seat to see the principal, I arrived at the check-in desk and asked for the waiting envelope. The older woman sitting there recognized me and smiled. "Here you go, Mrs. Williams."

"Thanks so much." A thought came to me, "Mrs. Barley, was Sherah Jones ever sent here to the office for getting into trouble?"

The woman looked around and leaned forward. "Just the time she exploded at the guidance teacher," she answered.

"Do you know what they argued about?"

She leaned closer and whispered, "She wanted to drop one of her classes, but the guidance teacher wouldn't let her. Said she needed the credits to pass."

Before I could ask which class Sherah had wanted to drop, there was movement behind us. "Mrs. Barley? Can you come into my office, please?" asked the principal. Her face turned pink at being caught gossiping. As I turned to face him, a reluctant half-smile crossed his face as he recognized me. "Mrs. Williams, have you been helped?"

"Yes, thanks. I just came to pick up the information that I'd requested." I turned away and left, feeling I was closer to another clue.

Walking to my car, I noticed Coach Johnson surrounded by a small group of students. He held a soccer ball, heading toward the sports field, followed by the students looking like groupies following a rock star. Isabella said he was popular with the students, and it was plain to see she was right.

I looked around, hoping I'd run into Evie Lynn by some miracle. But no luck, so I headed home. When I got there, Ditto was there to greet me. She often spent time next door with Isabella's dogs, so I never knew if she'd be waiting for me. Ditto seemed to be everybody's dog because she spent so much time between our two families. Ditto had a sweet personality, much less demanding than Sweet Pea, yet she couldn't take Sweet Pea's place in my heart even though I loved her dearly.

I picked her up, kissed her several times, and accepted licks from her. I carried her inside with me. With Mike gone until later, I planned to snuggle in with a glass of wine and a good movie with Ditto tucked beside me.

# CHAPTER 46

After seeing her kids off to school, Isabella dropped in the following morning to see me. I brewed some fresh coffee, and Mike joined us for his last coffee before heading out to work. He kissed the top of Isabella's head. "Your husband is a good man, Isabella. I'm happy he'll take over for me when I retire."

"I didn't know you were thinking about retiring, Mike," Isabella said, surprised.

"He's been making noises about it recently. Nothing definite yet," I quickly answered for him, unsure if I was ready for that change in our lifestyle.

"I don't want to wait so long that I'll be too old to travel. Your mother and I need to work out a few things before it's final, though." Looking at the time, Mike set his empty coffee mug down on the counter and came to kiss me goodbye before hurrying out.

"How did the meeting go with the financial advisor yesterday?" I asked Isabella.

It all came so naturally to her. Like a fish to water, she had taken to overseeing the Trust that Cal had left for us to run in memory of his birth mother. And she was good at it, making sound investment decisions, which had increased the bottom line for the Trust and ourselves.

In the contract we signed with Cal before he died, both Isabella and I would have a monthly income with the understanding that we would take the larger of the set salary or a percentage of the money invested. Isabella had done such an excellent job with investments that our monthly income was substantial, and I was grateful to have the financial security to live a somewhat indulgent lifestyle.

"We had a good discussion on how to diversify our funds. I'm still considering some options. After I pick out my choices, I'll review them with you for your approval. But it looks like we can expand the number of our safe houses."

"Great, good to know."

"So, Mama, how did your investigation of Mrs. Jones' murder go yesterday? What did you find out?"

After I filled Isabella in on what'd happened, I said, "We need to find out who Mrs. Jones argued with and why."

"If you think it's connected to Sherah, we must speak with her friends. Let's review the list and see how many we can talk to today."

We began filling out their profiles from the information and pictures on their Facebook page. We copied the top three girls' names on Ms. Greenly's list and their home addresses. Their activities seemed pretty standard, and nothing appeared out of line. Psychically, neither Isabella nor I sensed anything out of the ordinary.

We still wanted to interview Evie Lynn and Maria. I made up some ham and cheese sandwiches for lunch, and then we headed to the high school to see if we could catch either of the girls to interview. Now that we had their Facebook pictures, we might be able to catch them more easily.

I parked close to the student parking lot and waited until we heard the bell ring announcing the end of the school day. We got out of the car and separated, each going a different way. I walked to a spot where the students were loading into their vehicles. A loud voice to my side called out, "Maria! Wait up!"

A tall, lanky boy wearing thick eyeglasses passed before me, rushing toward a car about to pull out. I followed close behind him. I saw the Maria we were searching for as we approached the vehicle. Sensing something was happening, Isabella came hurrying over and blocked the car from pulling out while I pushed past the boy and leaned into the car. "Maria, don't go! I need to talk to you about Sherah. Please!"

"Yeah, my mother told me about you guys. I can't talk here, though." Looking at the boy, "Tommy, don't say a word to anyone about this, hear?"

"I won't. I promise," he vowed.

At my confused look, Maria added, "Tommy's my brother, and he knows I'll make his life miserable if he doesn't do what I say. Get in, Tommy! Hurry!"

"Where can we meet?" I asked.

"Follow me to the park beside my house. Do you know where it is?"

"Yes, I'll find it," I promised.

"Tell your friend to move so that I can leave." When I hesitated, she added, "Listen, I promise not to blow you off, okay? Now move! You're drawing attention."

I backed away from her car, as did Isabella. Then, we walked around the parking lot to make it seem like we were looking for someone else. After a few minutes of wandering, Isabella and I headed to our car and drove to meet Maria at the park.

True to her word, Maria was sitting in her car waiting for us. Tommy was nowhere in sight. He was close enough to his house that he had probably jogged home. When she saw us, Maria opened the car door and got out. She led us to an empty picnic table tucked to the side of the park and plopped down. Isabella and I joined her.

After introducing ourselves, I said, "Maria, we are looking for Sherah and need to find her before anything bad happens to her. What can you tell us about her being missing?"

"Are you guys cops?" she asked.

"No, we work independently for the police chief at times to find missing people. He's worried about Sherah's safety and asked us to help find her," Isabella said.

"Did you know that her grandmother was murdered?" I asked.

"Yeah, I heard. That sucks for Sherah, doesn't it?" Maria asked.

"It sure makes things difficult for her. What can you tell us about Sherah, Maria? Anything you can think of can help us," I said.

"It's between us, right? I don't want to be known as a snitch."

"Maria, did you notice a change in her behavior before she went missing?" Isabella asked.

Maria thought for a moment. "Yeah. Evie Lynn and I talked about it. Something was bothering her, and she seemed sad. We thought that maybe it was because her mother had missed her birthday, but Sherah said no when I asked her about it. We knew something was wrong, but she wouldn't tell us what it was. Evie Lynn's her best friend; maybe she knows something I don't."

"Can you think of anything that could have been bothering her?" I asked.

Maria shook her head.

"Well, you have our cell phone numbers. Please call us if you think of anything. Thanks for your time," said Isabella.

"Yes, thank you, Maria. We want to find Sherah and keep her safe," I added.

"I hope she's okay," she whispered sadly, walking back to her car with her head down.

We followed several steps behind her in silence, our hearts heavy with foreboding.

# CHAPTER 47

*II* Do you want to try to talk to Evie Lynn then?"
Isabella asked.

"I guess so," I responded without enthusiasm.

"What's wrong, Mama?" she asked, eying me. "You've been edgy all day."

"We're missing something right before us, aren't we?"

Isabella nodded in agreement. "But it'll come to us. We need more time to figure it out; that's all."

"We haven't got that luxury," I pushed back.

"I know, Mama." She took my hand. "What happened yesterday that has you so bothered?"

I looked her in the eye. "When I went to the school to pick up Sherah's class schedule, I was discussing it with Mrs. Barley, his secretary, when the principal interrupted our conversation and practically pushed me out of his office. Something about him doesn't sit right with me, and I don't trust him."

Isabella studied me. "I agree. I've been thinking about the murder of the young student several years back. I have a funny feeling it's somehow connected to Sherah being missing. We need to look into it. What do you say?"

"I think that's an excellent idea. Let's go see Roberto."

\*\*\*

When we arrived at the police station, the Chief was not there, and Isabella asked to see Margaret. Immediately, she came out to greet us and ushered us into the Chief's office for privacy.

"Can you check with the Chief and ask him if we can see the file folder on the murder of the high school student three years ago? I don't know her name," Isabella asked.

"The Chief told me long ago that whatever you girls want to review is alright with him. I know who you're talking about; sit here, and I'll be right back with her folder."

"I'll come with you, Margaret," Isabella said.

"Did Roger work on that case too?" I asked.

"I believe he did. He's here if you want to see him."

"That'd be great," I said.

"I'll send him in," she said before leaving with Isabella.

I remained sitting, and Roger entered the office in a few minutes. "What is it you wanted to see me about, Rosie?"

"We're going to review the file on that high school student murdered three years ago. Do you know the one?"

"Yeah, I don't think I'll be able to forget about it until we find out who killed her. It's one of those murders who won't leave me alone, you know?"

"Indeed, I do. What is it about that murder that won't let you rest?"

"She was strangled, and there were no signs of a struggle on her part—no skin beneath her nails, no extraneous bruises, no extreme trauma. And she wasn't drugged. She must have known her assailant, yet we came up with nada."

Isabella entered the office, grinning, holding a file box, and placing it on the table before me. Susan Suero's name was written on the side of the box, and I glanced at Roger. "Is this the girl?"

He nodded.

Lifting the top from the box, we looked inside to find a fat file folder and nothing else. I pulled it out and opened the file. Photos were piled on top, showing a beautiful young girl wearing a slightly surprised look as her long, curly hair splayed about her head like a generous-sized pillow. She was fully dressed and tidy, and her eyes were closed, but her body had begun to decay.

"She was a beauty," Isabella said. "Let's see what the notes say."

I divided them in half, handing Isabella her share, and we began to search through them. Roger said, "Let me know if you find something, okay?"

"Sure, Roger," I answered without looking up from the notes.

Isabella held a piece of paper out to me. "Look at this, Mama. Here's the notation on Principal Monahan. It agrees with what he told us."

I took the paper from her and read, "Principal Monahan ... said that the day before she disappeared, Susan had come to the office to speak to him about her problem. He told her she'd have to return because he had another

261

meeting with some parents. He said that was the last time he ever saw her."

"Nothing more on that? No follow-up?" I asked Isabella.

"Doesn't appear to be, Mama. Maybe we can talk to Susan's parents to see if they know her problem?"

"That sounds like a good idea. Is Susan's class schedule in the file folder? I don't have it here."

"It's not in my pile either. Do you think the school would have it?"

"I don't think so unless their software program allows for record-holding. We can check it out, though. I'll call Mrs. Barley right now and ask her."

"Good idea."

I called the school and was told Mrs. Barley was taking a few days off. I sat there trying to make sense of that. Suddenly, she was out of the office for a few days? During the middle of the week? Did it have something to do with our conversation the other day? Something wasn't right.

"What's wrong, Mama?"

I told Isabella what I'd learned. She shook her head in disbelief. "Something's off."

"I agree. Shall I call Susan's parents to see if they can talk to us?"

"Why not?" Isabella answered.

\*\*\*

Mr. and Mrs. Suero's house was in a lovely development on the west side of town. It was neat and landscaped beautifully, like all the lookalike houses on their street and most inside their gated community. When we pulled into the driveway, we were immediately greeted by Mrs. Suero's Schnauzer dog, who ran to us and wiggled around us with enthusiasm and curiosity. Then, the dog parked in front of me, forcing me to bend and pat her. Mrs. Suero laughed as she joined us. "Daisy does that to everyone until she gets enough attention. Come on, Daisy, come!" Mrs. Suero ordered. Daisy looked at me to see if I'd put up a fuss about her leaving me, and when I did nothing, she headed to her mistress and went inside through the opened door with her head bowed.

"Mrs. Suero? I'm Rosalie Williams, and this is my daughter, Isabella Bennett. We are the ones who called you earlier."

"Come in, come in. I've been expecting you."

The house was neat and cozy inside. As we followed her into the living room, we saw many pictures of Susan stacked amid others on the fireplace mantle. I was struck with sadness and wondered how any mother survives the excruciating pain of losing her child … especially if murdered. Indeed not easy to overcome.

"I've made some fresh iced tea. Can I get you some?" asked Mrs. Suero after settling us on her couch.

Isabella and I both nodded yes. After she left for the kitchen, I sought out Susan's pictures on the mantle. As I studied them, I felt a cool breeze, and her presence passed by me. I looked at Isabella to see if she'd felt it, too, and saw her shiver.

Mrs. Suero returned to the living room, holding a tray of drinks and a plate of tea cookies that looked and smelled freshly baked. "I try to keep as busy as possible to get through the dark days that come unexpectedly, even after all this time. Baking is one way for me to do that."

"The cookies look beautiful and smell divine. Thanks so much," I said as I reached for a cookie.

"So good," Isabella said after taking a bite of a cookie.

Mrs. Suero, sitting in the chair next to the couch, turned to us and asked with hope, "So, am I correct in that you ladies are looking into Susan's murder?"

"We're working with the police on something else, but we believe Susan's death might be related to the case we're working on. If it's not too difficult for you, we'd love to ask some questions about that time," Isabella said.

"It's been long enough, so I can talk about it without getting overly emotional. At this point, I'd do almost anything to discover the truth about what happened to Susan and why. I'd love to put the murderer behind bars."

"We would love that, too," I added.

"The thing that's been the hardest for me is to think about how Susan died without having a loving person at her side. And for the life of me, I can't figure out why anyone would want to kill her," she stated in disbelief.

"Can you lead us through the week before she died? Tell us any little detail you can think of—it doesn't matter how insignificant it may seem," Isabella urged.

Mrs. Suero was thoughtful. Then, she spoke, "Looking back now, I can see that Susan wasn't happy about something for longer than I originally thought at the time of her death. I asked her what was happening several times, and she said she'd handle the situation herself. She was angry at me for not thinking she was adult enough to take care of it herself."

"Any idea what was bothering her?" I asked.

"It was only after her death that I learned Susan had gone to the principal the day before she'd died and never did have the opportunity to discuss anything with him. I wasn't aware of what she wanted to talk to him about, though."

"Was she happy in all of her classes?" I asked.

"What do you mean?" Mrs. Suero asked.

"Was she perhaps looking to drop a class?" I pursued.

Mrs. Suero was quiet. "I overheard her say to one of her friends that she hated history. But I don't think she was considering dropping the class. That might be something for you to ask Donna Grayson, Susan's best friend back then. I don't know if Donna is still around, but I can give you her home address."

"That would be great," Isabella said.

A picture fell off the mantle startling us.

Mrs. Suero smiled. "Susan is letting us know she's around. I don't know if you believe in that, but I do. It's a great comfort for me."

"We believe in that, too," Isabella spoke up.

Out of my eye, I saw a shadow standing behind Mrs. Suero, stroking her hair. Unconsciously, Mrs. Suero pushed back her hair and patted it down. Isabella looked at me and winked, letting me know she could see Susan's shadowy spirit too.

After receiving Donna's address, we thanked Mrs. Suero and headed to our car. Daisy sat at Mrs. Suero's feet as she waved goodbye from the front entrance to the house.

It was too late to do much more that day. My head was spinning with bits and pieces of possible scenarios, and the best way of letting my brain sort things out was to spend a peaceful evening with Mike. It was the perfect way for me to unwind and relax. I knew it was the same for Isabella, so we parted with kisses when we arrived home, and each went our way.

# CHAPTER 48

❧ How are you this morning, darling girl?" I asked
Isabella as I handed her a cup of coffee.

"I have some news," Isabella grinned. "I tracked down
Donna Grayson last night and left her a voicemail to call
me regarding Susan. She called about an hour later, and
we talked for 30 minutes."

"That's great! What did she say?"

"She's had enough time to think about what was
happening back then, and she thinks Susan may have been
secretly meeting someone."

"Did she tell the police that?"

"No, Donna said she was so broken up about Susan's
murder that she couldn't think straight. Besides, it was just
a feeling, and she had no proof. But several times, Susan
didn't show up to study with her after school, and that
wasn't like her. When Donna asked her about it, Susan said

she was sorry but blew Donna off again, anyway. When I asked Donna to guess who the lover could have been, she said, 'Anyone, really.'"

"Okay. Let's see what we have so far," I suggested as I grabbed a piece of paper and wrote down:

- Susan Suero – high school student - murdered by strangulation – no unusual trauma.
- Did she know her assailant? – acted upset and told her mother she'd handle the problem– what was her issue? - Did she have a lover – who was it?
- Mrs. Jones – grandmother of Sherah, a high school student - murdered by trauma to the head – pushed – was it an accident? – was she trying to confront someone over Sherah's issue? – was she trying to protect Sherah? Protect her from what?
- Sherah – high school student - missing – hiding from Social Services - upset and unhappy at school – wanted to change one of her classes – which one? – why? Does she know who murdered her grandmother?

A vision came to me of her arguing with Coach Johnson. I dug out the photocopied class schedule for Sherah I'd picked up at the school two days before. "There's a question mark next to her history class. Do you suppose that's the class that Sherah wanted to change? So, if that's the class she wanted to change, is it because Coach Johnson made advances to her? Things are beginning to fall a bit more into place, don't you think?" I asked Isabella.

"I do indeed. It wouldn't be the first time a male teacher has gotten out of line with his students. I think it's time we met with Evie Lynn— whether she wants to meet with us or not."

"I agree. Let's go," I said.

*\*\*\**

Instead of becoming conspicuous by going inside Joe's Pizza to wait for Evie Lynn to show up, we sat in the parking lot to wait for her. We ducked our heads below the dashboard when we saw a worn, somewhat tattered car pull into the parking lot. After we peeked out and saw her leaving her car, we dashed toward her, blocking her from escaping us.

"Evie Lynn, please wait! We need your help! Please tell us where we can find Sherah."

Ticked off that we had caught her off guard, annoyance flashed on her face. Scowling, she demanded, "Get away from me! I don't have anything to say to you two. Out of my way!"

"Look, we're not interested in turning Sherah over to Social Services, honest! We have to get in touch with her before anything bad happens to her. But we need your help!"

Evie Lynn huffed and began to turn away. Isabella grabbed her arm, jerking her back toward us. "Look, Evie Lynn, if you truly love your friend and want to keep her safe, hear what we have to say, okay?" pleaded Isabella.

Evie Lynn was quiet as she studied Isabella. "Maria told me that you've already talked to her. I don't have anything more to tell you."

"Maria said that you are Sherah's best friend ..."

"Yeah, so?"

"So, we think her running away isn't about Social Services. We think she was having trouble with Coach Johnson. Are we right?" asked Isabella.

"You know about that?" asked Evie Lynn in amazement.

"We can only help her if we can find her. Do you know where she's hiding?" I interjected.

"I'm not sure," she answered honestly.

"What do you mean, not sure?" I asked, trying to rein in my disappointment.

"Sherah and I keep in touch by phone, but she won't tell me where she's staying because she doesn't want to get me in trouble with the police. But," she frowned, "I think she has to be with one of her Grandmother's friends."

Relief poured over me. "And who might that be?"

"I don't know, but I heard a dog barking in the background the last time I talked to her if that helps."

"Hey, Evie Lynn, are those women bothering you?" yelled a masculine voice from the back door of Joe's Pizza.

"Nah, they're just asking for directions," she hollered back. "You'd better get going. My boss doesn't like anyone keeping us from our jobs."

"When you talk to Sherah next, please tell her we want to help her. Here's a card with both our names and numbers on it. Tell her to call us anytime, day or night," Isabella urged. "And thanks for your help."

As Evie Lynn hustled through the open door that her boss held open for her, we headed back to our car. I turned to Isabella, "We're getting closer."

She nodded and smiled. "I think you're right." Just then, Isabella's phone rang. It was Joslin. "Hi, sweetie. We're on our way. We'll pick you up right out front as usual. See you in a few minutes."

# CHAPTER 49

**▮▮** Hi, sweetheart. Are you okay?" I asked when I saw the unhappy look on Joslin's face.

"No, I'm *not* all right," Joslin answered grumpily.

"What's wrong?" I asked.

"Oh, Gramma Rose, it was so embarrassing! I had a vision in English class and screamed out loud, 'Don't touch me!' The teacher thought I was yelling at the cute new boy sitting next to me in my class. I had to explain that I had been daydreaming to her and everyone else. Now the new boy thinks I'm a real jerk … as well as the whole class."

"I'm so sorry, honey," Isabella said.

"Me, too," I said.

We remained silent in the car, each sorting through what'd happened with Joslin at school. Being psychic can be challenging at times. It wasn't easy to have visions pop into your head so real that you could smell, taste, and see every nuance within a scene, seeming more real than life itself. Joslin was so sensitive psychically that until she learned to have better control, visions could take over and become problematic for her. We'd need to work with her in that regard. I looked back at her with sympathy.

"Do you want to tell us about the vision you had?" I asked. I sighed.

Joslin closed her eyes and remained still. She fidgeted in the back seat for several minutes. Finally, she said, "I think it was about the girl you're looking for."

"Take hold of my hand," I urged, knowing that if we connected, I might be able to see what she was seeing. As soon as our hands were clasped, I was thrown into a whirlwind and saw myself looking on as Coach Johnson was trying to pull Sherah close to him. She kept saying, "Don't touch me! Get away from me!"

As Coach Johnson continued to advance and reached his hand toward her, Sherah threatened, "I'm telling on you."

He sneered. "You forget something. I'm the teacher, and no one will believe what you say—a nothing little girl who's always trying to get attention with the short skirts she wears. You've brought this on yourself."

"No, I haven't," she yelled, tears in her eyes. "You're the one … not me!"

"Who is going to believe you, huh?"

Suddenly, Joslin pulled her hand from mine, and I found myself falling into the present time, more than a bit undone from what I'd seen.

Joslin exclaimed, "It was so real! What is going to happen to her?"

During the vision, Isabella had grabbed my other hand to have seen enough for herself to know what we'd seen. "It depends on whether Gramma Rose and I can locate Sherah and ensure she is protected," Isabella said.

"Who was that man?" asked Joslin.

"I think that is something your mother and I should keep to ourselves so we don't involve you," I answered.

"The less you know, the better," Isabella agreed.

"What about Sherah? I'm scared for her; I think that man is looking for her," Joslin said.

"Did you see anything else? Do you know where she's hiding?" I asked Joslin, curious to know if she had seen beyond what I had.

"Nope, not right now," she sighed, unhappy.

Isabella dropped me off at home. I would call the churches in Sherah's grandmother's neighborhood to see if I could locate her friends through the pastor or priest there. I was sure her church would be one of the two closest to her house—close enough to walk to.

Two hours later, I was utterly worn out. I'd learned about the history of the two churches closest to Sherah's grandmother's house from the pastor and the priest, not sparing a word about their place of worship. The time had been well spent since I had three different names and addresses of women considered Mrs. Jones' friends. I didn't want to call them, perhaps alerting Sherah that we were on to her, forcing her to keep running. I listed the names of those I thought might be hiding Sherah. Isabella and I would track each down tomorrow. I only hoped that both the priest and the pastor would keep their word to remain quiet about my inquiries.

During the night, I tossed and turned to the point that Mike stirred and asked, "What is it, Rosie? Are you okay?"

"So sorry, honey, I'm just trying to work things out in my head. I don't mean to keep you from sleeping."

"Okay, sweetheart, as long as you're okay. Try to get some sleep, though, hear?"

"Yes, I will. I promise," I said as I kissed Mike on the cheek.

I laid back against the pillows and closed my eyes. Something wasn't making sense. If Coach Johnson was sexually involved with some of the young girls at school and had been for any length of time, how was he getting away with it? Who was protecting him and why? Any behavior like that can't stay hidden forever—someone had to know.

I turned onto my side to sleep with that thought in mind and rested uncomfortably for the night.

# CHAPTER 50

A fter Mike left for work the following day, I called Isabella and told her what I'd learned from researching Sherah's grandmother's friends. "Let's wait until school starts before we visit these women. Why don't you join me for a cup of coffee, and we'll leave soon afterward?"

"Sounds good. I'll see you after Joslin and the boys leave for the bus," Isabella answered. "It will be such a relief if we can locate Sherah and help her out of her mess."

Soon, Isabella popped through the doorway, and it was clear that something was wrong. "What is it, Isabella?"

"I had a vision, Mama, and it was bad. I think I know what happened to Susan ... and I think I know who might have killed her."

"What do you mean?"

"We think that Coach Johnson is the cause for Sherah's being missing. So, doesn't it make sense that he could have also been involved in Susan's death?"

I nodded.

"Also, Mama, if Coach Johnson has been harassing girls for a long time and nothing has come of it, who's covering for him? He couldn't have hidden his behavior without help, right?"

"My thoughts exactly. I tossed and turned all night thinking about it," I said.

"Did you notice Principal Monahan's car the other day when we were at the school? Do you know what it is?"

"No, sweetheart, I'm not really into cars."

"It's a Porsche Boxster, Mama! It's an older model, but still … the new sports cars are close to $100,000. Where would he get that kind of money?"

"So, what are you saying? Principal Monahan is blackmailing Coach Johnson? What did you see in your vision?"

"I saw the two of them fighting. I think they were fighting over money. If sexual indiscretions are nothing new for Coach Johnson, it makes sense that Principal Monahan could be blackmailing him. And if Susan threatened to make their actions public, it stands to reason that either one of them might be the one to have killed her."

When Isabella's words were out of her mouth, a glass flew off the counter and crashed to the floor. Both Isabella and I jumped, spooked by the sudden crash and the glass splintering across the floor. "Susan, are you letting us know we're on the right track?" I whispered.

"Wow, I've hit on something alright," Isabella said.

"How does Sherah's grandmother fit into it?" I asked.

"I'm not sure, but if we can talk to Sherah, maybe she can tell us."

"Okay, then, let's go find Sherah after I clean up this mess," I urged. "I don't want Ditto to step in it and get hurt."

\*\*\*

We drove to the neighborhood where Sherah's grandmother lived and parked the car. Her three friends were within walking distance, although several blocks apart.

The first two houses we visited yielded nice older friendly women who were shaken and saddened about their friend's untimely death. They had nothing but good things to say about their friend and how much Sherah's grandmother loved her granddaughter, glad to provide for her. Neither had a dog, and we soon bade them goodbye and walked to the last house on our list. It was the one I'd circled, farthest from Sherah's grandmother's house.

We stood on the porch of a tidy but old, worn house and knocked on the front door. The curtains in the window to the right of the door pulled back enough for us to see dark eyes peering at us. After several minutes, the door cracked open, and a small, frail voice, hard to hear over a small dog barking at her heels, asked, "What do you want?"

Isabella and I had already made up a story about wanting input on funeral arrangements for Sherah's grandmother. So, I asked, "Mrs. Walters, here's our card. We want to talk to you about Mrs. Jones and some arrangements we're making for her funeral."

"Isn't that up to the family?" she questioned.

"Yes, normally it is. However, since no family member has stepped forward, we've talked to the pastor about doing something at the church for her."

"That'd be nice," she said.

"Can we come in to discuss it in more detail, Mrs. Walters?"

"Well ..."

"We won't take up much of your time."

The dog pushed her way outside and danced at our feet.

"No, Bella! Come here right now!" demanded Mrs. Walters, opening her door wider for the dog to return. "Bad dog. Well, I guess you might as well come inside, too," she grumbled.

As soon as we sat down, the dog was at our feet, barking and holding a toy in her mouth, waiting for us to throw it for her. Mrs. Walters became frustrated with the dog and said, "Sherah, come get Bella."

When Sherah entered the room and saw us, she rushed to the front door to escape. Isabella, sitting nearest the door, was faster and blocked her way. Sherah began to push Isabella away, trying to escape, but Isabella held fast. "Sherah, we're here to help. Please listen to what we have to say."

"Get out of my way!" Sherah yelled, trying to get around Isabella.

Mrs. Walters stood up and hollered, "Stop! What is going on here?"

I stepped toward Isabella and Sherah, still in their standoff positions, and placed my hand on Sherah's shoulder. "We know about Coach Johnson, Sherah. We're here to help you. Please listen to what we have to say."

Those words floating in the air took all the wind out of Sherah, and she crumbled into a mass of tears. I reached for her and held her in my arms, surprised that she allowed me to do so. I thought how difficult it must be for her to be hiding in fear, not knowing how she would get out of the trouble that she was in, especially with a future that looked so dim.

Once Mrs. Walters understood what was happening, she turned into the sergeant-in-arms, barking orders. Meekly, we followed what she said and sat in the places she pointed out to us. "Sherah, let the ladies speak. It seems they can help us, and we need their help."

"Before we start, I have one question," I began. "Sherah, did your grandmother tell the principal what was happening with you and Coach Johnson?"

Tears filled her eyes and trailed down her face. "I don't know. I told her not to get involved and warned her not to go to the school. But I think that's maybe what happened, and now she's dead," she sobbed. "All because of me!"

Isabella looked at me and nodded in understanding. "Did you talk to anyone about what was happening with you and Coach Johnson?" asked Isabella.

"Only Evie Lynn," Sherah mumbled.

"Not Maria?" I asked.

Sherah shook her head. "No."

"Do you know of anyone else Coach Johnson may have been harassing?" I asked.

"There's a new girl that just moved here. She's timid, and he asked her to stay after one day last week. She didn't look too happy about it."

"What's her name?" Isabella asked.

"Sally Broadmore or Blackmore, I think. Something like that."

"Okay, here's what we need you to do. Stay here with Mrs. Walters, and don't go out. You must stay hidden until Isabella, and I put the pieces in place to turn in Coach Johnson. Do you both understand how important it is for Sherah to stay hidden?"

Mrs. Walters nodded.

"Are you going to tell Social Services and the police where I am?" asked Sherah.

Isabella and I shook our heads and said in unison, "No!"

A look of relief crossed Sherah's face. "Okay, I'll do as you say. I don't have much choice," she lamented with a deep sigh.

"Good girl," I said.

We sat and spoke with Mrs. Walters while Sherah sat quietly beside her, listening to our conversation. "Until we have Coach Johnson in custody, it is important to keep Sherah inside and not let anyone—even her closest friends—know she is here with you," Isabella said.

Mrs. Walters nodded in understanding.

"You have our telephone numbers, and you can call us anytime. Any questions before we leave?" asked Isabella.

"How long do you think my hiding will take place?" Sherah asked.

"As long as it takes," I said honestly. Seeing Sherah's frustration, I hurriedly added, "which we're hoping will be just a few days."

"I sure hope so," Sherah said.

"C'mon, dearie, let's say goodbye to these lovely ladies, and then I'll fix you some lunch," Mrs. Walters said to Sherah before leading us to the door.

# CHAPTER 51

O utside, Isabella looked at me expectantly. "I hope you have a plan for trapping Coach Johnson since Sherah thinks this will all be wrapped up in a few days."

"I do. Let me run it by you to see what you think," I said, smiling.

I explained what I had in mind as we walked the block or two back to our parked car. Isabella looked doubtful. "I'm not sure this is such a good idea. Let's run this by Chief Roberto."

"Okay," I agreed. "Let's see if he's in."

As we entered the police headquarters, Margaret greeted us at the front. "The Chief will be with you shortly. Can I get you something to drink? Coffee? Water?"

"Yes, water would be wonderful," I said.

Isabella said, "No, thank you, Margaret."

Fifteen minutes later, Chief Roberto came out to the front. "Sorry about the wait. Come on into my office, and we can talk there."

We shared our ideas with him about what'd happened to Susan, Sherah's grandmother, and Sherah's reason for hiding without telling him where she was hiding. He was impressed. "So, what's your plan?"

After I told the Police Chief what I had in mind, he didn't dismiss it altogether. "Let me get this straight. You want to send a threatening note to Coach Johnson and Principal Monahan, each telling him that you know his dirty secrets and will go to the police unless he makes it worthwhile?" Roberto asked. "Blackmail each of them?"

"Yes, that's the idea," I said.

"And you are asking them to meet you at a location where the police can hide in wait to arrest them?"

"Yes, that's the idea," I concurred. "And Isabella and I want to be there."

"If I decide to go ahead with the idea. I'm not going to be responsible for putting you in danger. Got that?"

"Okay," I said, "but we want to be there when you charge them and take them off to jail."

"We'll see about that. I want to run this idea by Mike and Sammy." At the dismay on our faces, he added, "Sorry, ladies, but I want their input about this before I do anything."

"We still want to be there to watch it all go down, though," insisted Isabella.

"Understood," Roberto responded.

"Sorry, Chief, but you're needed out front," Margaret said as she stood in the doorway.

"Okay, ladies, we'll catch up later," Roberto said as he rose from his seat and herded us out of his office.

"You'll let us know as soon as possible, right?" I asked, turning to him before we headed out the door.

Roberto held his thumb up before turning to the man waiting to speak with him.

I excitedly grabbed Isabella's hand as we walked to the car to head home. "This will work out; I just know it is."

Isabella was quiet. "I hope so, Mama."

\*\*\*

Later that afternoon, Mike and Sammy walked through the door as Isabella and I finished the notes threatening Coach Johnson and Principal Monahan.

"Roberto said you think Coach Johnson is the one who killed Susan and is harassing Sherah?" Mike asked.

"Yes, and there's more to tell you," Isabella said.

"What's that?" asked Sammy.

"If Coach Johnson has been doing his dirty deeds for a while now, there has to be someone protecting Coach Johnson, right? We think it may be Principal Monahan. And he may have been involved with Sherah's grandmother's death."

"How did you two come up with that?" Mike asked.

We shared our thoughts with the two of them, and like Roberto, they were impressed.

"Rosie, I don't like the idea of either of you being involved in this crazy scheme you've come up with to blackmail Coach Johnson and Principal Monahan. It's too dangerous," Mike ordered.

"It's a great idea, and it'll work!" I protested.

"Roberto said he'd consider us being there when the shoe dropped on them, as long as we're in the background, and we want to be there," Isabella added.

"That's not going to happen," challenged Sammy.

"I think we should at least discuss it," I said.

"There's nothing to discuss," Mike said, brushing us off.

Mike's stubbornness about this was unusual, although he'd become even more protective of me lately. I wondered if it was because we were aging, and he felt more vulnerable and less in control. Realizing there was no sense in arguing with him, I remained silent.

Sammy looked at Mike and said, "Well, it might be something we'd consider once all the plans are in place."

Mike thought about what Sammy had said, "Maybe," he responded.

"We've written the notes already," Isabella said as she handed the papers to Sammy.

"YOU ARE A MURDERER. I HAVE PROOF. COME ALONE TO FLOYD LAMB STATE PART THURSDAY AT 10 P.M. AND LEAVE $20,000 CASH IN SMALL BILLS ON THE FIRST COVERED PICNIC TABLE OR I'LL GO TO THE POLICE. MAKE SURE YOU'RE NOT FOLLOWED."

"Why there?" Mike asked, curious.

"Since the park closes at 8 p.m., there shouldn't be anyone around at that time, don't you think?" I asked.

"Yeah, it should be empty by then," Mike agreed. "Sammy and I are meeting with Roberto tomorrow. We'll let you know if he decides to proceed with this."

Isabella and I looked at each other. Psychically, we'd seen it moving forward. The understanding passed between us that we'd talk with Roberto again about being there that night. He thought the world of us, and I knew we could talk him into it.

# CHAPTER 52

E xcitement and nervousness filled me as Thursday night approached. Much to our husbands' disappointment, Roberto felt we'd earned the right to be at the park that night when they arrested Coach Johnson and Principal Monahan. Although we didn't have living proof that Coach Johnson had killed Susan, we felt her spirit surrounding us, encouraging us we were on the right track. With his highly developed intuition, Sammy felt Susan's spirit, too, causing him not to doubt us.

When Thursday night arrived, and it was time to leave, I walked to Isabella's house next door. The twins were now old enough to be alone and watch over Joslin. Isabella was hollering up the stairs to her kids. "Goodbye, kids. You can check in with Mrs. Smith in the guest house if needed. Love you."

Ever since Cal had left his house to Isabella, she'd used the guest house as a "holding tank" for women trying to escape their abusive relationships. All the guests were called Mrs. Smith or Mrs. Jones, so no true identity was leaked to the outside world.

Muffled goodnights flowed down the stairs. "Good night," and "Bye."

Isabella turned to me. "All set?"

"As ready as I'll ever be, I guess," I answered, suddenly feeling unsure. I'd missed something. What was it? Worry began to grow in me, and I tried to shake it off as we loaded into Isabella's SUV.

When we got to the park, we hid our car in the trees off to the side of the road so that it wouldn't be noticed and hiked down toward the front entrance to join the others waiting for the two men to show up.

The minutes ticked slowly by, and I reached the point of wanting to scream to break the tension in the air. Isabella was anxious, and I saw her looking around in concern. "What is it, Isabella?" I whispered.

"Something's wrong. Do you feel it?"

"What do you mean?" I asked.

"I don't know, but something is off," she whispered as we heard a truck pull into the park.

The truck hesitated for a minute and then slowly veered to the left, heading to the first covered picnic table. The driver's door opened, and the man behind the wheel remained there, searching the area before moving to get out of the truck. The night lights that brightened the entrance to the park made it barely possible to see that it was Coach Johnson dressed in a dark hoody with his face primarily covered. He stepped down from the truck and yelled, "Anyone here?"

When no one responded, he hollered, "If you're here, come on out now! I won't hurt you; I just want to talk to you."

All was quiet. Roberto had made it clear that for Coach Johnson and Principal Monahan to be arrested, it'd be best to have them there with the money easily in sight, tying them to the threats in their notes. I held my breath, and my heart sank, knowing something was wrong. This wasn't the way I'd envisioned it. Why was Coach Johnson expecting to talk to someone? He was supposed to be dropping off money, that was all.

I felt someone sidle up to where Isabella and I were standing. Both Isabella and I jumped with fright and stifling screams. My heart stopped when I saw that it was Joslin! What was she doing here? How did she get here? I remembered when Isabella said goodnight to her children before we'd left. There had been only two responses—not three like there should have been. That was what had caused my unease at that time, and I'd missed it.

Lifting a finger to her mouth, Isabella whispered, "What are you doing here?"

"I heard you and Gramma Rose talking about coming here tonight, and I wanted to see if the man you are after is the same one that I saw in my vision ... the man who was mean to Sherah."

"How did you get here?" I whispered, unable to hold back my curiosity.

"I hid in the back of the car. You never noticed me," she said, smiling at her cleverness.

"Shh, be quiet. Stand right next to me and don't move," ordered Isabella, annoyed. Looking over at me, she shook her head in disbelief at Joslin's shenanigans.

Next, Principal Monahan's sports car pulled in and parked along the far side of the truck out of our view. Coach Johnson approached the principal behind the car's wheel and bent to talk to him. His voice was loud enough for us to hear. "What are you doing here? Is this about wanting more money?"

"What are you up to now? Is this some trick, Coach?" roared the principal. He got out of his car and approached Coach Johnson, unafraid, walking into the light. He poked his finger at the coach's chest and demanded, "Why did you send me that note and drag me out here?"

Joslin was intently studying Principal Monahan, who had turned our way. With his face now easily visible, Joslin put her hands together and cupped them around my ear. She whispered, "That's not the right man, Gramma Rose."

"It's not?" I asked softly.

Joslin shook her head.

The two men stood arguing and yelling at each other. When Coach Johnson turned toward the light, Joslin came alive when she saw who it was. Before we could stop her, she yelled, "That's him! That's him, Mama, and Gramma Rose, the one in my vision. Don't let him get away!"

Isabella missed grabbing Joslin's arm as she raced forward, yelling, "Don't let him get away!"

Surprised to see her there, no one moved for a second or two. Then Principal Monahan sprang forward. Moving quickly, he grabbed Joslin, holding her tight against him with his arm around her neck in a chokehold.

"Everyone, back off, or the kid will get hurt."

Joslin's eyes filled with tears, and she began to panic. She was having a hard time breathing, and she struggled against him. She was angled away from the group who'd come crashing through the undergrowth and surrounded the picnic area, held in position by the principal's threat, making it impossible for anyone to understand that her squirming was her wanting air. Her lips were becoming blue, and no one was coming to her aid. I raced out of our hiding place and pushed into Principal Monahan. I lifted my knee and rammed it into his groin, making him fold over in agony, loosening his arm around Joslin's neck. She fell to the ground like a limp doll, painfully sucking in the air.

While Principal Monahan struggled with pain, he stretched his arm and knocked me alongside my head. I felt a sharp pain; that was the last thing I remembered before I blacked out.

When I came to, arrests were in process, and an ambulance had been called for Joslin and me. We were taken to the hospital, and once the doctor checked us over, we were ordered to spend the night there so that they could keep an eye on us. We shared a double room which Mike, Sammy, and Isabella soon filled. They were determined to spend the night with us, not letting us out of their sight. I don't think they trusted us not to get into more trouble. I overheard Mike tell Sammy he'd have his hands full with Joslin taking after her Gramma Rose.

*** 

The next few days were a blur, and things fell into place as the news came out that Coach Johnson and Principal Monahan were arrested. Under pressure, both came clean about the deaths they had caused, both insisting that neither had been intentional and bartered for no death penalty.

In a fit of anguish and anger, Coach Johnson had choked Susan to death when she wanted out of their short sexual relationship and threatened to tell her parents about him. Principal Monahan had walked into the coach's room where they'd just argued, and the body was still warm. Fast thinking led Principal Monahan to make his proposal to keep quiet for money which, according to the coach, gave him no choice but to go along with the arrangement.

Principal Monahan confessed that Sherah's grandmother had come to see him about Coach Johnson's behavior toward Sherah. He'd not been in the office at the time of her arrival and her subsequent leaving. When he returned several minutes later and learned she'd been there, wanting to speak with him, he sensed he knew why. Principal Monahan left the school and walked to where he could see her in the distance, making her slow journey home, and confronted her. She angrily got into his face about Sherah's situation, and without even thinking about the consequences, he pushed her away from him, never intending to hurt her, according to him.

Susan's parents were saddened but grateful to have the mystery of their daughter's death come to light. Her mother called and told us that on Thursday night, around the time of Coach Johnson's arrest, all of Susan's photos on the mantle fell off in one full sweep to the ground as Susan's spirit celebrated her release. With a teary voice, she said, "Thank you for letting my daughter rest in peace."

Sherah's news was even brighter. She was welcomed back to school, and her friends were there to support her. Her grandmother's friend, Mrs. Walters, made arrangements with Social Services to keep Sherah living with her. With the sale of her grandmother's house, Sherah would have enough money for college if she was careful how it was invested. Mrs. Walters was already working with an accountant to help with that.

Joslin had not entirely escaped from the drama she'd experienced at the park. She'd had a rude awakening to what could happen if she reacted without thinking more about the consequences of her actions. In that way, I knew Joslin was like me, poor thing. But she was also clever and strong and could overcome what life presented. She was a survivor with a large heart, and I didn't feel a constant need to worry about her.

Isabella and I had accomplished everything we had hoped for on this last assignment we'd worked together. I had promised Mike that there would be no more of my work for Roberto. He said he was too old to survive another case of my playing detective.

We'd talked more about Mike retiring, and we agreed that it was time for him to turn over the reins of the business to Sammy. It was also time for us to begin to travel and enjoy our later years together. And, after this last escapade, I couldn't agree more.

# CHAPTER 53

A few days later, I answered the phone to Jack's excited voice asking, "Is Dad there with you, Mom?"

"Not far away. Why?"

"Good. Get him and put us on speakerphone, okay? We have some news."

I called Mike, and he came to my side. "Hey, Jack, what's going on?"

"Sarah's here with me. We wanted to tell you that we got married last night."

Mike and I were stunned and remained silent.

"Did you hear me?" asked Jack, worried.

"That's wonderful!' we gushed together. I held back my disappointment in not being there to see Jack get married, but that was soon dismissed with his following news.

"Sarah didn't want a traditional wedding, so we decided to get married first and then have the reception later. Are you busy this weekend?"

I looked at Mike and laughed. "Of course, we'll make arrangements to come for the celebration. Do Karen and Coyote know your news?"

"Not yet. They're our next call. Here's the bride; she wants to say hello."

"Hi, Auntie Rose and Uncle Mike. Ooh, that's now going to change, isn't it?"

"Why not make it easy on yourself and simply call us Rosie and Mike? We love having you as our daughter-in-law, Sarah. We've wanted this for some time now."

Mike cut in, "Welcome to the family, Sarah. We love you."

"Thank you, eh, Rosie and Mike. I love you too. Here's Jack."

"Mom and Dad, thank you for pushing me to stick to my guns with Sarah, and I want you to know how happy I am."

"I'm happy for you, son," Mike said, tears filling his eyes.

"See you soon, Dad. I love you."

Mike was too overwhelmed to reply.

"Tell Karen to call me after you talk to her, okay?"

"Will do, Mom. Love you."

"We love you, too."

After I hung up the phone, Mike and I smiled at each other.

\*\*\*

Jack and Sarah's reception out at the ranch where they were living now was beautiful in its simplicity. The guests who attended were the younger sister-friends (Isabella, Nica, and Angela) and their families and loved ones, Karen, Coyote, Romano, Randy, Virginia, Maria, Miguel, and their family, Maggie and David Brooks (Sammy's parents) and, of course, Mike and me. Some of Jack and Sarah's friends showed up, adding to the celebration.

I bit back a smile as I watched Romano struggling not to take over the barbequing of the ribs and other treasures cooking over the coals. Randy was at his side, arguing quietly to let Jack do it unless asked.

I went to stand by Jack and whispered, "Romano would love to take over this job if you'd let him."

He looked at me in surprise. "Really? Great! Where is he?"

Soon, Randy and I watched Romano in his glory, turning the ribs and smiling at everyone, happy to be in charge of the grill. I turned to Randy, "You've got to hand it to him; Romano sure does love to cook."

"And eat," laughed Randy. Then, he leaned into me, kissing me on the cheek. "Now that you and Mike are alone, what will you two do?"

"Well, that is the question now. Mike has been working on something with Dave but hasn't told me what he has in mind yet."

"I'm sure you'll find out soon enough. I know it'll be good," Randy said with a twinkle in his eyes and a smug smile.

"You know what he's planning, don't you?" I asked, already knowing the answer.

"Now, Rosie, you know I can't say anything, so I will change the subject. Jack told me that he and Sarah will work together at the ranch and expand it for wayward boys. That's quite an undertaking."

"Jack has wanted to turn the ranch into a boys' retreat since he bought the place. Now that the paperwork and licenses are complete, it makes sense for them to work together as they did for many summers volunteering on the reservation."

A clanking of silverware tapping on glass became louder and louder as the demand for the groom to kiss the bride increased. I watched Jack and Sarah passionately kiss and then whisper something between them. I sought out Karen, and when I found her, she looked at me with tears and a broad smile. I blew her a kiss.

Beyond her, I saw a shadow move toward Jack and Sarah. My heart raced when I recognized Tom Little Horse's spirit. As Jack's birth father, he wore a proud expression as he placed his hands on each of their shoulders. Jack jerked in surprise and searched for me. When our eyes met, I smiled and nodded, validating what'd happened.

Mike came to my side. "I'm so proud of our son. Thank you so much for making him mine."

"He was always meant to be yours, handsome," I said, pulling him closer and kissing him tenderly.

"I know. Grandmother told me he was my blessing."

"Did she, now? What a wise woman she was," I smiled.

The truth was that we both were blessed to have Isabella and Jack as our children this lifetime, and we were grateful. Each time we saw them and our hearts lifted, it was evident. It doesn't get better than that, and we know it.

THE WORLD.

# CHAPTER 54

**B**ack in Las Vegas, I was at loose ends, not knowing what to do. I saw my tarot cards lying on top of my desk, and I picked them up. It had been quite a while since I had used them. But I was curious to see what the future held for me since I hadn't a clue. Mike still had not said a word about what he was planning. I chose just one card from the deck instead of the usual three, giving the card's meaning greater significance.

I shuffled the cards for many minutes, asking for the best card to describe my future. Finally, I laid the cards out and studied them for a moment. I closed my eyes and let my hand hover over the cards until I lowered it and touched one, pulling it toward me.

I turned it over and laughed out loud when I saw what it was … the World card, the best card in the deck as far as I was concerned. Its meaning is fulfillment, achievement, and completion. It also represents an ending to a cycle of life, a pause in life before the next big cycle—an indicator of a significant and unstoppable change.

Looking at the World card, I felt an overwhelming love for Mike because he meant the world to me in many ways. So far, we'd had a beautiful, loving life together, and because of him, I was looking forward to what lay in wait for us as a couple in the winter of our lives. I felt the breeze from my grandmother's spirit floating by. Her words flowed to me. *"I love surprises, don't you, Rosie girl?"*

"Yes, and I love you too, Gram," I whispered to the air around me.

Ditto barked and raced to the door. Mike was home. I heard him coming down the hallway toward me. He peeked in at me from the doorway of the office. "Hi, sweetheart. I've made reservations at Rosalie's tonight for 6 o'clock. Dave and Maggie will be joining us. I hope that's okay with you."

"That sounds wonderful. Is there anything special going on I should know about?"

"You'll have to wait and see," he answered mysteriously with a smile.

Earlier, I'd seen Mike lay out his sports jacket, button-down shirt, and tie, making a concerted effort to dress up more. I later donned one of Louie's designer outfits, which I found to my dismay, to be a bit snug. I refused to name my expansion as usual, "middle-age bulge." I'd need to get back on schedule for my exercise classes.

As I descended the stairs, my heart fluttered when I saw Mike standing at the bottom, watching me with such love that he took my breath away. "Ahh, my queen, still so beautiful after all these years."

I smiled, warmed by his words.

Mike stepped close at the bottom of the stairs, pulling me into a kiss so sweet and passionate that I protested when he stopped. "More," I whispered. "I want more, handsome."

"And, so you shall, my queen."

Standing there kissing like teenagers made me laugh out loud, causing him to join me. "C'mon, sweetheart, let's get a move-on. We don't want to be late for Dave and Maggie."

I was always proud when I saw my name adorning the beautiful restaurant. Romano and Mimi had christened their restaurant after me, and I was forever grateful. Rosalie's was named one of the top three places to dine in Las Vegas, and Romano's expertise in the kitchen had kept it there since the beginning.

We were no strangers to the restaurant and were greeted by name and immediately ushered to a small, intimate nook in the back of the dining room. Maggie and Dave were already there. With the vast grin he was wearing, Dave looked like the cat that had swallowed a canary. Maggie looked at me with a puzzled look. "Do you know what's going on?" she whispered as I sat beside her.

"Not a clue. You?"

"Nothing."

Immediately, our glasses were filled with Perrier water since all the staff knew that was what we preferred. The sommelier came to our table and presented a bottle of champagne to Mike for approval. "Compliments of the chef."

Mike went through the routine of wine tasting, and then our flutes were filled. He looked at Dave, who nodded his approval. "Dave and I have come up with an idea we'd like to present to you ladies."

299

"Yes?" asked Maggie.

"What is it that you two have been cooking up?" I asked.

Dave took over. "Since Mike and I both are retired now and want to travel with our beautiful brides, we thought you two might like this," he said, handing us each a brochure for the Oceania cruise line with its "Around the World in 180 days" tour. "It touts 92 destinations across 44 countries."

"It sounds exhausting," I said without thought, causing Maggie to laugh.

"We thought that too initially," Mike said somewhat defensively. "But once you see how the visits are laid out and spaced, you'll be able to see how it is accomplished without it becoming too much. Besides, with us staying in the owner's suite we've booked, we will be pampered and rested. It's a small ship with under 800 passengers, so attention is given to even the smallest details to make this a special trip."

Seeing how excited Mike, Dave, and Maggie were about the trip, I laughed joyfully. "It sounds wonderful! When do we push off, mates?"

As Maggie and I chattered excitedly about what we couldn't wait to see, Mike and Dave watched us, satisfied with their gift choice. I knew that alone made it worth their effort.

\*\*\*

Later, as Mike and I lay together in bed, I was quiet—both excited and undecided about what this trip represented to me.

"A penny for your thoughts," whispered Mike as he held me tight, my head resting on his shoulder.

"The trip is wonderful; you and Dave couldn't have come up with anything better. I guess I'm trying to sort out the emotions that taking this trip has brought up," I said softly.

"What do you mean, sweetheart?"

"Our whole lives have changed. You're retired now. The kids have their own families, and the Trust is being run beautifully without my help. Yes, we're free from many responsibilities, but I feel that with us floating around the world on that boat, we could lose ourselves and miss out on living a critical part of life," I said.

Mike was quiet, lost in thought. Then he spoke. "There is a time and season for everything. Since I met you, Rosie, you have felt responsible for others. And in doing so, there have been many times where you've gotten involved in situations and gotten hurt. Now it's time for you to experience life in a different, gentler way by relaxing and enjoying life for what it is now. That is what I hope this trip will help you do," he murmured, stroking my hair.

I was still, thinking about what his words meant. "Mike?" I whispered in a small voice. "I don't like getting old. I like being needed and in the thick of things."

Mike rose on his elbows, looking at me with concern. "My beautiful queen, you are always needed. I need *you* as much as the air I breathe." I watched as his eyes glistened with tears. Then he leaned closer and whispered, "I want you to know that if I have to do this whole life thing again, I'll search the world for you, Rosie. "

With tears, I spoke my truth, "And I'll be waiting for you…."

The vision of the World card flashed before me, and I smiled, knowing without a doubt that the next cycle of our lives together would be just as wonderful as when we were younger. I felt my grandmother's spirit around me, and her words floated in the air, *"And so it will."*

# ACKNOWLEDGMENTS

Many thanks to all those in my family and others who have supported me on my journey of writing mysteries. It's heartwarming to have your encouragement.

I thank all of you who picked up my books to read. I hope you enjoyed every chapter and, even more so, found my books challenging to put down. That's what a good mystery is all about.

I thank you from the bottom of my heart for all my ARC readers and those who have taken the time to review my books on various sites.

I was blessed the day I contacted Kelly Martin to be my book cover designer. Thank you, Kelly, for your creativity and artistic talents. I love your work—and you.

Thank you, Jake Naylor, for designing my website, being my layout person, and my "everything" to do with my writing. I don't know what I'd do without you and your marvelous talent. I love you.

# BOOKS BY J.S. PECK

**THE DEATH CARD SERIES**
- Book 1: *Death on the Strip*
- Book 2: *Death at the Lake*
- Book 3: *Death Returns*
- Book 4: *Death Waits*
- Book 5: *Death in the Shadows*
- Book 6: *Death Comes Calling*

- *Angels Out of the Dark*
- *The Waiting Room* (due out 2022)

# BOOKS BY JOAN S. PECK

- *The Seven Major Chakras – Keeping it Simple*
- *A Simple Approach to Living a Successful Life*
- *What You Need to Know to Live a Spiritual Life*
- *Prime Threat – Shattering the Power of Addiction*

# J.S. PECK

Joan was reared in a family of readers in small-town Elmira, New York. Each Sunday afternoon was a special time when each family member could relax with a good book. She was raised to be opened-minded, and discussion about her beliefs was encouraged. Joan understood that we are all connected energetically and can communicate with others who have passed on. Drawn to her spiritual and supernatural beliefs, Joan brings that idea into her writings and expresses her interest in shattering the power of addiction and human sex trafficking.

Joan is an editor and author of short stories, spiritual books, novels, and a mystery book series called The Death Card Series. Her book, *Angels Out of the Dark*, delves into human sex trafficking and is a book every person needs to read. Her book, *Prime Threat - Shattering the Power of Addiction*, has helped many looking to understand addiction in a whole new way.

Joan is also a contributing writer for several magazines and serves as the Editor in Chief for *Chic Compass* magazine, produced in Las Vegas and available worldwide.

She lives in Las Vegas, Nevada, with her dog, Sweet Pea, one of the main characters in the Death Card Series.

Sign up for my newsletter and download Death on the Strip for Freebies and Up-to-Date News for FREE. https://mailchi.mp/8d7e97110d71/deathcard

Check out my web page, joanspeck.com, for information on all my books, a complete list of books in order, and my spiritual blogs.

**Don't forget to follow me on:**

- **Twitter:**
  https://twitter.com/JoanPeck

- **Facebook:**
  https://www.facebook.com/DeathCardSeries

- **Instagram:**
  https://www.instagram.com/death_card_series/

- **BookBub:**
  https://www.bookbub.com/profile/j-s-peck

- **Goodreads:**
  https://www.goodreads.com/author/show/18191647.J_S_Peck

*If you enjoyed reading this book and the entire Death Card series, please help other readers discover it by sharing your thoughts in a review. Thanks so much!*